Lady Georgiana Fullerton

Too Strange not to Be True

A Tale: Vol. I.

Lady Georgiana Fullerton

Too Strange not to Be True
A Tale: Vol. I.

ISBN/EAN: 9783337080082

Printed in Europe, USA, Canada, Australia, Japan

Cover: Foto ©Andreas Hilbeck / pixelio.de

More available books at **www.hansebooks.com**

TOO STRANGE NOT TO BE TRUE.

VOL. I.

TOO STRANGE NOT TO BE TRUE.

A TALE.

BY

LADY GEORGIANA FULLERTON,

AUTHORESS OF
'ELLEN MIDDLETON,' 'LADYBIRD,' ETC.

IN THREE VOLUMES.

VOL. I.

LONDON:
RICHARD BENTLEY, NEW BURLINGTON STREET.
1864.

INTRODUCTION.

In the following tale, the scene of which is laid in countries, and amidst persons, whose language was not our own, there has been no attempt to adopt the phraseology of the epoch over which these events extend. There did not seem any particular object in rendering the thoughts and conversations of German and French people in the English of the eighteenth, rather than of the nineteenth, century.

Truth and fiction are closely blended in this tale, and in the Appendix will be found the materials from whence some of its incidents have been drawn—as also the narrative which has furnished its ground-work. Those who are sometimes glad to turn away for a while from the beaten roads of history, and to tread the bye-ways of romance—who love truth which resembles fiction, and fiction which follows closely in the footsteps of truth—may, perhaps, find some little interest in this story of the last century.

> ' Full of hope, and yet of heart-break ;
> Of the here, and the hereafter.'
>
> *Legend of Hiawatha.*

TOO STRANGE NOT TO BE TRUE.

PART I.

CHAPTER I.

The woods! O solemn are the boundless woods
  Of the great western world when day declines;
And louder sounds the roll of distant floods,
  More deep the rustling of the ancient pines,
When dimness gathers on the stilly air,
  And mystery seems on every leaf to brood:
Awful it is for human heart to bear
  The weight and burthen of the solitude.

Mrs. Hemans.

White she is as Lily of June,
And beauteous as the silver moon,
When out of sight the clouds are driven,
And she is left alone in heaven.
    *   *   *   *
I did not speak—I saw her face:
Her face! it was enough for me!
I turned about, and heard her cry,
'O misery! O misery!'   Wordsworth.

In the earlier part of the last century,
through one of the primeval forests of the New
World, northward of the region which the

French colonists called the Eden of Louisiana, a man was walking one evening with his gun on his shoulder, followed by two dogs of European breed, a spaniel and a bloodhound. The rays of the setting sun were gilding the vast sea of flowers lying to his right beyond the limits of the wood through which he was making his way, impeded every moment by the cords of the slender liana and entangled garlands of Spanish moss. The firmness of his step, the briskness of his movements, the vigour of his frame, his keen eye and manly bearing, and above all the steady perseverance with which he pursued the path he had chosen, and forced his way through all obstacles, indicated a physical and moral temperament well fitted to cope with the many difficulties inherent to the life of a settler in the Nouvelle France.

Henri d'Auban had been a dweller in many lands—had lived in camps and in courts, and held intercourse with persons of every rank in most of the great cities of Europe. He was thirty-five years of age at the time this story opens, and had been in America about four years. Brittany was his native country; his parental home a small castle on the edge of a cliff overlooking one of the wildest shores of that rude coast. The sea-beach had been his playground; its weeds, its shells, its breaking waves, his toys; the boundless expanse of the ocean and its great ceaseless voice, the endless theme of his secret musings; and the pious legends of the Armorican race, the nursery tales he had heard from his mother's lips. Brittany, like Scotland, is 'a meet nurse for a poetic child,' and her bold peasantry have retained to this day very much of the religious spirit of their forefathers. Early in life Henri d'Auban lost both his parents—the small-pox, the plague of that epoch in France, having carried them both off within a few days of each other. He saw them buried in the little churchyard of Keir Anna, and was placed soon after by some of his relations at the college of Vannes, where he remained several years.

On leaving it he began life with many friends, much youthful ambition, and very little fortune. Through the interest of a great-uncle, who had been a distinguished officer in Marshal

Turenne's army, he was appointed military attaché to the French Embassy at Vienna, and served as volunteer in some of the Austrian campaigns against the Turks. He visited also in the Ambassador's service several of the smaller courts of Germany, and was sent on a secret mission to Italy. On his way through Switzerland he accidentally made acquaintance with General Lefort, the Czar of Muscovy's confidential friend and admirer. That able man was not long in discovering the more than ordinary abilities of the young Breton gentilhomme. By his advice, and through his interest, Henry d'Auban entered the Russian service, advanced rapidly from post to post, and was often favourably noticed by Peter the Great. He seemed as likely to attain a high position at that monarch's court as any foreigner in his service. His knowledge of military science, and particularly of engineering, having attracted the sovereign's attention on several occasions when he had accompanied General Lefort on visits of military inspection, the command of a regiment and the title of Colonel were bestowed upon him. But just as his prospects appeared most brilliant, and his favour with the Emperor was visibly increasing, he secretly left Russia and returned to France. Secrecy was a necessary condition of departure in the case of foreigners in the Czar's service. However high in his favour, and indeed by reason of that favour they were no longer freeagents— his most valued servants being only privileged serfs, bound to his dominions by laws which could only be evaded by flight—permission was hardly ever obtained for a withdrawal, which was considered as a sort of treason.

Colonel d'Auban's abandonment of the Russian service excited the surprise of his friends. Some painful thoughts seemed to be connected with the resolution which had cut short his career. He disliked to be questioned on the subject, and evasive answers generally put a stop to such enquiries. He had, however, reached an age when it is difficult to enter on a new career; when old associations on the one hand, and youthful competitors on the other, stand in the way of a fresh start in life. After six or seven years' absence from his country, he scarcely felt at home in France. His acquaintances thought him changed. The eager ambitious youth had become a quiet thoughtful man. But if the enthusiasm of his character was subdued, its energy was in no wise impaired. Youthful enthusiasm, in some natures, simply evaporates and leaves nothing behind it but frivolity; in others, it condenses and becomes earnestness.

At this turning moment one of the insignificant circumstances which often influence a person's whole destiny directed Colonel d'Auban's thoughts to the New World. In Europe, and especially in France, a perfect fever of excitement was raging on the subject of colonisation. The rich territories on the banks of the Mississippi seemed a promised land to speculators of all classes and nations. The eagerness with which Law's system was hailed in Paris, and the avidity which sought to secure a share in the fabulous prospects of wealth held out to settlers in the New France, had never known a parallel. This fever was at its height when one day the ex-favourite of the Czar happened to meet in the Luxembourg gardens an old school-fellow, who, the instant he recognised his comrade at

Vannes, threw himself into his arms, and poured forth a torrent of joyful exclamations This was the Vicomte de Harlay, a wealthy, good-natured, eccentric Parisian, who had employed his time, his wit, and his means, since he had come of age, in committing follies, wasting money, and doing kindnesses. He had already managed to get rid of one large fortune ; but fortune seemed to have a fancy for this spendthrift son of hers, and had recently bestowed upon him, through the death of a relative, a large estate, which he seemed bent upon running through with equal speed.

'My dear d'Auban! I am delighted to see you! Are you come on a mission from the polar bears? or has the Czar named you his Ambassador in Paris?'

' I have left the Russian service.'

' You don't say so! Why people declared you were going to cut out Lefort and Gordon. Have you made your fortune, dear friend?'

D'Auban smiled and shook his head. ' A rolling stone gathers no moss.'

' Do you wish to make your fortune?'

' I should have no objection.'

' What are you doing, or wishing to do?'

'I am looking out for some employment. A small diplomatic post was offered to me some time ago, but it would not have suited me at all. I wish I could get a consulship. I want hard work, and plenty of it. What an extraordinary being you must think me.'

'Have you anything else in view at present?' enquired De Harlay, too eagerly bent on an idea of his own to notice his friend's last observation.

'No. When a person has thrown himself out of the beaten track, and then not pursued the path he had struck out, it is no easy matter to retrace his steps. Every road seems shut to him.'

'But don't return to the beaten track—to the old road. Come with me to the new France. My cousin M. d'Artagnan is commandant of the troops at New Orleans, and has unbounded influence with the governor, M. Perrier, and with the Company. I will introduce you to him. I know he wants men like you to come out and redeem the character of the colony, which is overrun with scamps of every description.'

'Amongst whom one might easily run

the risk of being reckoned,' said d'Auban, laughing.

'Nonsense,' cried his friend. 'I am turning emigrant myself, and have just obtained a magnificent concession in the neighbourhood of Fort St. Louis, and the village of St. François.'

'You! And what on earth can have put such a fancy in your head?'

'My dear friend, I am weary of civilisation —tired to death of Paris—worn out with the importunities of my relations, who want me to marry. I cannot picture to myself anything more delightful than to turn one's back, for a few years, on the world, and oneself into a hermit, especially with so agreeable a companion as M. le Colonel d'Auban. But really, I am quite in earnest. What could you do better than emigrate? A man of your philosophical turn of mind would be interested in studying the aspect of the New World. If the worst came to the worst, you might return at the end of a year and write a book of travels. I assure you it is not a bad offer I make you. I have considerable interest in the Rue Quincampoix.

I was invited to little Mdlle. Law's ball the
other day, and had the honour of dancing a
minuet with her.   I shall write a *placet* to
the young lady, begging of her to obtain
from Monsieur son Père a concession for a
friend of mine.   It would be hard if I could
not help a friend to a fortune when Laplace,
my valet—you remember him, don't you?—
has made such good use of our visits to the
Paris Eldorado that the rogue has set up his
carriage.   He was good enough when he met
me trudging along in the mud on a rainy day
to offer me a lift.   It is evident the world is
turned upside down, on this side of the globe
at least, and we may as well go and take a
look at the *revers de la médaille*.   Well,
what do you say to my proposal?'

'That it is an exceedingly kind one, De
Harlay.   But I have no wish to speculate or,
I will own the truth, to be considered as an
adventurer.   That you, with your wealth,
and in your position, should emigrate, can be
considered at the worst but as an act of folly.
It would be different with me.'

' Well, I do not see why the new France is
to be made over to the refuse of the old one.

I see in your scruples, my dear friend, vestiges of that impracticability for which you were noted at College. But just think over the question. Nobody asks you to speculate. For a sum not worth speaking of you can obtain a grant of land in a desert, and it will depend on your own ability or activity whether it brings you wealth or not. There is nothing in this, I should think, that can offend the most scrupulous delicacy.'

'Can you allow me time to reflect?'

'Certainly. I do not sail for six weeks. It is amusing in the meantime to hear the ladies lamenting over my departure, and shuddering at the dangers I am to run in those wild regions, where, poor dears, they are dying to go themselves, and I fancy some of them believe that golden apples hang on the trees, and might be had for the trouble of gathering them, if only *le bon Monsieur Law* would let them into the secret. Have you seen the line of carriages up to his house? It is the very Court of Mammon. Duchesses and marchionesses jostle each other and quarrel on the staircase for shares, that is when they are happy enough to get in, which is not

always the case.   Madame de la Fère ordered
her coachman to drive her chariot into the
gutter and overturn it opposite to his door.*
Then she screamed with all her might, hoping
the divinity would appear.   But the wily
Scotchman was up to the trick, and ate his
breakfast without stirring.   We who were in
his room almost died of laughing.   Well,
good bye, my dear Colonel.   When you have
made up your mind let me know, that I may
bespeak for you in time a berth in the Jean
Bart and a concession in the New World.'

The Vicomte de Harlay walked away, and
d'Auban paced for a long time the alleys of the
Luxembourg, revolving in his mind the ideas
suggested by this conversation. 'After so
many doubts, so many projects which hàve
ended in nothing, how singular it would be,'
he said to himself, 'if a casual meeting with
this scatter-brained friend of mine should end
in determining the future course of my life.'
He had never thought of emigrating to the
New World, but when he came to consider it
there was much in the proposal which harmo-
nised with his inclinations.   The scope it

* A fact.

afforded for enterprise and individual exertion was congenial to his temper of mind. Above all, it was something definite to look to, and only those who have experienced it know what a relief to some natures is the substitution of a definite prospect for a wearying uncertainty. In the evening of that day he called at one of the few houses at which he visited—that of M. d'Orgeville. He was distantly related to this gentleman, who held a high position amongst what was called the parliamentary nobility. His wife received every night a chosen number of friends, men of learning and of letters, members of the *haute magistrature*, dignitaries of the Church, and women gifted with the talents for conversation, which the ladies of that epoch so often possessed, frequented the salon of the Hotel d'Orgeville, and formed a society little inferior in agreeableness to the most celebrated circles of that day.

Does it not often happen, unaccountably often, that when the mind is full of a particular subject, what we read or what we hear tallies so strangely with what has occupied us, that it seems as if a mysterious answer were given to our secret thoughts? When d'Auban took his place that evening in the circle which surrounded the mistress of the house, he almost started with surprise at hearing M. de Mesme, a distinguished lawyer and scholar, say—

'I maintain that only two sorts of persons go to America, at least to Louisiana—adventurers and missionaries: you would not find in the whole colony a man who is not either an official, a priest, a soldier, or a scamp.'

'A sweeping assertion indeed,' observed Madame d'Orgeville. 'Can no one here bring forward an instance to the contrary?'

'The Vicomte de Harlay has turned concessionist, and is about to sail for New Orleans. In which of the four classes he has mentioned would M. de Mesme include him?' This was said by a young man who was sitting next to d'Auban.

'Exceptions prove the rule. M. de Harlay's eccentricities are so well known that they baffle all calculation.'

'For my part,' said M. d'Orgeville, 'I cannot understand why men of character and ability do not take more interest i these new colonies, and that the objects of a settler in that distant part of the world should not be considered worthy the attention of persons who have at heart not only the making of money, but also the advancement of civilisation.'

'Civilisation!' ejaculated M. de Mesme, with a sarcastic smile. 'What a glorious idea the natives must conceive of our civilisation from the specimens we send them from France!'

'Surely,' exclaimed young Blanemenil, d'Auban's neighbour, 'M. Perrier, M. d'Artagnan, the Père Saoel and his companions, are not contemptible specimens of French merit?'

'Officials, soldiers, priests, every one of them,' retorted M. de Mesme.

'What I have not yet heard of is a concessionist a planter, an *habitant* who is not a mere speculator or a needy adventurer. I appeal to you, M. Maret. Does not your brother write that the conversion of the Indians would be comparatively easy did not the colonists, by their selfish grasping conduct and the scandal of their immoral lives, throw the greatest obstacles in the way of the missionaries? Did he not add that a few honest intelligent laymen would prove most useful auxiliaries in evangelising the natives?'

'Your memory is faithful, M. de Mesme. I cannot deny that you quote correctly my brother's words. But his letters do not quite bear out your sweeping condemnation of the French settlers. If I remember rightly, he speaks in the highest terms of M. Koli and M. de Buisson.'

'Is it the Père Maret that Monsieur is speaking of?' asked d'Auban of Madame d'Orgeville.

'Yes, he is his brother, and the missionary priest at St. François des Illinois. M. Maret is Monsigneur le Prince de Condé's private Secretary. Let me introduce you to him. Perhaps you may have seen his brother at St. Petersburg before the expulsion of the Jesuits?'

'I knew him very well, and wished much to know where he had been sent.'

'It may then, perhaps, interest you, sir, to read the last letter I have received from my

brother; it contains no family secrets,' M.
Maret said with a smile.

This letter was dated from the Illinois. It
did not give a very attractive picture of
the country where d'Auban had already travelled in imagination since the morning. It
made it evident that Europe sent out the
sum of her population to people the New
World; and that if good was to be done in
those remote regions, it must be by an unusual
amount of patience, courage, and perseverance.

But what would have disheartened some
men proved to d'Auban a stimulus. There
were, he perceived, two sides to the question
of emigration; the material one of profit—
the higher one well worthy of the attention
of a Christian. It seemed to him a singular
coincidence that, on the same day on which
it had been proposed to him to emigrate to
America, a letter should be put into his hands,
written from that country by a man for
whom he had a profound respect and attachment. He found in it the following passage:

' The excellence of the climate, the beauty
of the scenery, the easy navigation of the

river, on the shore of which our mission is situated, and which flows a little below it into the Mississippi, the extreme fertility of the soil, the ease with which European productions grow and European animals thrive here, make this village quite a favoured spot, and one peculiarly adapted for the purposes of French colonisation. But whether such establishments would be an advantage to our mission, is extremely doubtful. If these emigrants were like some few I have known, men of religious principles and moral lives, nothing could be better for our Indians, or a greater consolation to us, than that they should settle in our neighbourhood; but if they are to resemble those who, unfortunately, have of late years been pouring into Louisiana—adventurers, libertines, and scoffers—our peaceful and edifying Indian community would be speedily ruined. The Indians are very like children. Their powers of reasoning are not strong. What they see has an unbounded influence over them. They would quickly discover that men calling themselves Christians, and whom they would look upon as wiser than themselves, set at nought the principles of the Gospel, and, in spite of all the missionaries might say or do, the effect would be fatal. From such an evil as that I pray that we may be preserved.' *

When the visitors had taken their leave that night, and d'Auban remained alone with his friends, he opened his mind to them and asked their advice. M. d'Orgeville hesitated. His wife, a shrewd little woman, who understood character more readily than her excellent husband, fixed her dark penetrating eyes on Colonel d'Auban, and said, 'My dear friend, my opinion is that you will do well to go to the New World. I say it with regret, for we shall miss you very much. If, indeed, you had accepted the heiress I proposed to you, and advanced your interests by means of her connections, it might have been different; but a man who at thirty years of age refuses to marry an heiress foolish enough to be in love with him, because, forsooth, he is not in love with her—who does not accept a place offered to him because it would happen to break another man's heart not to get it, and who

* From the *Lettres édifiantes*.

will not make himself agreeable to the Regent's friends because he thinks them, and because they are, a set of despicable scoundrels—my dear Colonel, such a man has no business here. He had better pack up his trunks and go off to the New World, or to any world but this. Tenderness of heart, unswerving principles, the temper of Lafontaine's oak, which breaks and does not bend, do not answer in a country where everyone is scrambling up the slippery ascent to fortune, holding on by another's coat.'

'And yet,' answered d'Auban, 'there are men in France whose noble truthfulness and unshaken integrity none venture to call in question;' and as he spoke he glanced at M. d'Orgeville.

'True,' quickly answered his wife, laying her hand on her husband's embroidered coat-sleeve; 'but remember this, such men have not their fortunes to make. They are at the top of the ladder, not at the bottom, and that makes all the difference. It is always better to look matters in the face. Here you have —some people say wantonly—I am persuaded for some good reason—but anyhow you have

turned your back upon fortune in a most
affronting manner, and the fickle goddess is
not likely, I am afraid, to give you in a
hurry another opportunity of insulting her.
I really think you would be wrong to refuse
M. de Harlay's proposal. You see, my dear
friend, you are not a practical man.'

'Well, I will not urge you to define that
word,' said d'Auban, with a smile; 'but if
your accusation is just, how can you believe
that I shall triumph over the difficulties of a
settler's life?'

'Oh, that is quite a different affair. What
I call a practical man in Europe is one who
bends before the blast, and slips through
the meshes of a net. In the desert, and
among savages, the temper of the oak may
find its use, and stern self-reliance its element.'

'I am afraid she is right,' said M. d'Orgeville, with a sigh; 'though I would fain not
think so.'

'At any rate, you will not be in a
hurry to come to a conclusion on this important question, and if you do emigrate, all
I can say is, that you will be a glorious

instance of the sort of settler M. de Mesme does not believe in.'

A few weeks after this conversation had taken place, M. de Harlay and Henri d'Auban were watching the receding coasts of France from the deck of the Jean Bart, and four or five years later the latter was crossing the forest, on his way back to the Mission of St. Francis, after a visit to an Indian village, the chiefs of which had smoked the pipe of peace with their French neighbours. He had learnt the language, and successfully cultivated the acquaintance of many of the native tribes, and was at the head of a flourishing plantation. Madame d'Orgeville had proved right. The peculiarities of character which had stood in the way of a poor *gentilhomme* seeking to better his fortunes in France, favoured the successful issue of his transatlantic undertakings. M. de Harlay had fulfilled his promise by obtaining from the Company a grant of land for his friend adjacent to his own concession, and he had worked it to good purpose. His small fortune was employed in the purchase of stock, of instruments of labour, and, it must be

owned, of negroes at New Orleans. But it
was a happy day for the poor creatures in
the slave-market of that city, when they
became the property of a man whose principles and disposition differed so widely from
those of the generality of colonists. He engaged also as labourers Christian Indians of
the Mission, and a few ruined emigrants, too
happy to find employment in a country
where, from want of capital or ability, their
own speculations had failed. It was no easy
task to govern a number of men of various
races and characters, to watch over their
health, to stimulate their activity, to maintain peace amongst them, and, above all, to
improve their morals. The Indians needed
to be confirmed in their recently acquired
faith, the negroes to be instructed, and the
Europeans, with some few exceptions, re-
called to the practice of it. He laboured
indefatigably, and on the whole successfully,
for these ends. His courage in enduring privations, his generosity, perhaps even more his
strict justice, his kindness to the sick and
suffering, endeared him to his dependants.
He seemed formed for command. His out-

ward person was in keeping with his moral qualities. He hunted, fished, and rode better than any other man in the Mission or the tribe. In physical strength and stature he surpassed them all. This secured the respect of those unable to appreciate mental superiority.

It was not extraordinary, under these circumstances, that his concession thrived, that fortune once more smiled upon him. He was glad of it, not only from a natural pleasure in success, but also from the consciousness that, as his wealth increased, so would his means of usefulness. He became deeply attached to the land which was bountifully bestowing its treasures upon him, and displaying every day before his eyes the grand spectacle of its incomparable natural beauties. His heart warmed towards the children of the soil, and he took a lively interest in the evangelisation of the Indian race, and the labours of the missionaries, especially those of his old friend Father Maret, whose church and the village which surrounded it stood on the opposite bank of the stream, on the side of which his own house was built. If his life had not been one of incessant labour, he must have suffered from its loneliness. But he had scarcely had time during those busy years to feel the want of companionship. Month after month had elapsed in the midst of engrossing occupations. On the whole, he was happy — happier than most men are—much happier, certainly, than his poor friend, M. de Harlay, who wasted a large sum of money in building an *habitation*, as the houses of the French settlers were called, totally out of keeping with the habits and requirements of the mode of life he had adopted. For one whole year he tried to persuade himself that he enjoyed that kind of existence; it was only at the close of the second year of his residence in America that he acknowledged to his companion that he was bored to death with the whole thing, and willing to spend as large a sum to get rid of his concession as he had already expended upon it. At last, he declared one morning that he could endure it no longer.

Maître Simon's barge was about to descend the Mississippi to New Orleans. The temptation was irresistible, and he made up his mind to return to France, leaving behind him his land, his plantations, his horses, and the charming *habitation*, called the *Pavillon*, or sometimes, ' *La Folie de Harlay*.' D'Auban, he said, might cultivate it himself, and pay him a nominal rent, or sell it for whatever it would fetch to some other planter. But in America he would not remain a day longer if he could help it, and if Monsieur Law had cheated all the world, as the last letters from Paris had stated, the worst punishment he wished him was banishment to his German settlement in the New World. And so he stood, waving his handkerchief and kissing his hand to his friend, as the clumsy barge glided away down the giant river ; and d'Auban sighed when he lost sight of it, for he knew he should miss his light-hearted country-man, whose very follies had served to cheer and enliven the first years of his emigration. And, indeed, from that time up to the moment when this story begins, with the sole excep-tion of Father Maret, he had not associated with anyone whose habits of thought and tone of conversation were at all congenial to his own. No two persons could differ more in character and mind than De Harlay and himself; but when people have been educated together, have mutual friends, acquaintances, and recollections, there is a common ground of thought and sympathy, which in some measure supplies the place of a more intimate congeniality of feelings and opinions.

He sometimes asked himself if this isolation was always to be his portion. He had no wish to return to Europe. He was on the whole well satisfied with his lot, nay, grateful for its many advantages; but in the course of a long solitary walk through the forest, such as he had taken that day, or in the evenings in his log-built home, when the wind moaned through the pine woods with a sound which reminded him of the murmur of the sea on his native coast, feelings would be awakened in his heart more like yearnings, indeed, than regrets. In many persons' lives there is a past which claims nothing from them but a transient sigh, breathed not seldom with a sense of escape—phases in their pilgrimage never to be travelled over any more —earthly spots which they do not hope, nay, do not desire to revisit—but the remembrance of which affects them just because it belongs to the dim shadowy past, that past which was once alive and now is dead. This had been the case with d'Auban as he passed that evening through the little cemetery of the Christian Mission, where many a wanderer from the Old World rested in a foreign soil by the side of the children of another race, aliens in blood but brethren in the faith. A little farther on he met Thérèse, the catechist and schoolmistress of the village. He stopped her in order to enquire after a boy, the son of one of his labourers, whom he knew she had been to visit. Thérèse was an Indian girl, the daughter of an Algonquin chief, who, after a battle with another tribe, in which he had been mortally wounded, had sent one of his soldiers with his child to the black robe of St. François des Illinois, with the prayer that he would bring her up as a Christian. He had been himself baptised a short time before. The little maiden had ever since been called the Flower of the Mission. Its church had been her home; its festivals her pleasures; its sacred enclosure her playground. Before she could speak plainly she gathered flowers and carried them

in her little brown arms into the sanctuary
When older, she was wont to assemble the
children of her own age, and to lead them
into the prairies to make garlands of the
purple amorpha, or by the side of the
streams to steal golden-crowned lotuses from
their broad beds of leaves for our Lady's altar;
and under the catalpa trees and the ilexes she
told them stories of Jesus and of Mary, till
the shades of evening fell, and " the compass
flower, true as a magnet, pointed to the north."
As she advanced in age her labours extended;
but such as her childhood had been, such
was her womanhood. She became the catechist of the Indian converts, and the teacher
of their children. The earnest piety and the
poetic genius of her race gave a peculiar
originality and beauty to her figurative language; and d'Auban had sometimes concealed
himself behind the wall of the school hut and
listened to the Algonquin maiden's simple
instructions.

' How is Pompey's son to-day? ' he asked,
as they met near the church.

' About to depart for the house of the great
spirits,' she answered. ' He wants nothing

now; angels will soon bear him away to the land of the hereafter. We should not grieve for him.'

' But *you* look as if you *had* been grieving. Thérèse, do not hurry away. Cannot you spare me a few minutes, even though I am a white man? I am afraid you do not like French people.'

' Ah! if all white men were like you it would be well for them and for us. It is for one of the daughters of your tribe that I have been grieving, not for the child of the black man.'

' Indeed, and what is her name?'

' I do not know her name. She is whiter than any of the white women I have seen— as white as that magnolia flower, and the scent of her clothes is like that of hay when newly mown.'

' Where did you meet with her?'

' I have seen her walking in the forest, or by the side of the river, late in the evening; and sometimes she sits down on one of the tombs near the church. She lives with her father in a hut some way off, amongst the white people, who speak a harsher language than yours.'

'The German colony, I suppose? Is this woman young?'

'She must have seen from twenty to twenty-five summers.'

'When did they arrive?'

'On the day of the great tempest, which blew down so many trees and unroofed our cabins. A little boat attached to Simon's barge brought them to the shore. They took shelter in a ruined hut by the side of the river, and have remained there ever since.'

'Have they any servants?'

'A negro boy and an Indian woman, whom they hired since they came. She buys food for them in the village. The old man I have never seen.'

'And why do you grieve for this white woman, Thérèse?'

'Because I saw her face some nights ago when she was sitting on the stump of a tree, and the moon was shining full upon it. It was beautiful, but so sad; it made me think of a dove I once found lying on the grass with a wound in her breast. When I went near the poor bird it fluttered painfully and flew away. And the daughter of the white

man is like that dove ; she would not stay to
be comforted.'

'Does she ever come to the house of
prayer ? '

'No. She wanders about the enclosure
and sits on the tombstones, and sometimes
she seems to listen to the singing, but if she
sees anyone coming she hurries off like a
frightened fawn.'

' And her father, what does he do ? '

' He never comes here at all, I believe.'

' And you think this young woman is unhappy ? '

'Yes.   I have seen her weep as if her eyes
were two fountains, and her soul the spring
from whence they flowed.   It is not with us
as with the white people.   We do not shed
tears when we suffer.   The pain is within,
deep in the heart.   It gives no outward sign.
We are not used to see men and women
weep.   One day I was talking to Catherine,
a slave, on the Lormois Concession, who
would fain be a Christian, but that she hates
the white people.   Many years ago she was
stolen from her own country and her little
children, and sold to a Frenchman.   There

are times when she is almost mad, and raves
like a wild beast robbed of its young. But
Catherine loves me because I am not white,
and that I tell her of the Great Spirit who was
made man, and said that little children were to
come to Him. I was trying to persuade her
to forgive the white people and not to curse
them any more, and then, I said, she would
see her children in a more beautiful country
than her own, in the land of the hereafter;
that the Great Spirit, if she asked Him,
would send His servants to teach them the
way to that land where mothers and children
meet again if they are good. Then in my ear
I heard the sound of a deep sigh, and turning
round I saw the white man's daughter, half-
concealed by the green boughs, and on her
pale cheeks were tears that looked like dew-
drops on a prairie lily. Her eyes met mine,
and, as usual, she was off into the forest before I could utter a word. I have not seen
her since.'

' I wish you did know her,' said d'Auban,
thoughtfully.

Thérèse shook her head.

' It is not for the Indian to speak comfort

to the daughter of the white man. She does not know the words which would reach her heart. The black robe, the chief of prayer, whom the Great Spirit sends to His black, His Indian, and His white children ; His voice is strong like the west wind ; from His lips consolations flow, and blessings from His hand. And you, the eagle of her tribe, will you not stoop to shelter the white dove who has flown across the Great Salt Lake to the land of the red men ?'

D'Auban felt touched by the earnestness of Thérèse's manner, and interested by her description of the stranger. He could easily imagine how desolate a European woman would feel on arriving in such a miserable place as the German settlement, and he promised that as soon as he could find leisure he would ride to that spot and see if he could be of use to the white man's daughter. Upon this they parted, but the whole of the evening, and the next day in the maize fields and the cotton groves, his imagination was continually drawing pictures of the sorrowful woman— the wounded bird—that would not stay to be comforted.

CHAPTER II.

He is a proper man's picture, but . . . how oddly he is
suited. I think he bought his doublet in Italy, his round hose
in France, his bonnet in Germany, and his behaviour every-
where.—*Shakespeare.*

> The power that dwelleth in a word to waken
>   Vague yearnings, like the sailor's for the shore,
> And dim remembrances whose hues seem taken
>   From some bright former state, our own no more.
> The sudden images of vanished things
> That o'er the spirit flash, we know not why,
> And the strange inborn sense of coming ill
> That ofttimes whispers to the haunted breast,
> Whence doth that murmur wake, that shadow fall?
> Whence are those thoughts?   ' 'Tis mystery all.'
>   *Mrs. Hemans.*

A FEW days after his conversation with
Thérèse, d'Auban rode to a place where
some Saxon colonists were clearing a part of
the forest. He wished to purchase some
of the wood they had been felling, and, dismounting, he tied his horse to a tree and
walked to the spot where the overseer was
directing the work. Whilst he was talking
to him, he noticed an old man who was

standing a little way off, leaning with both
hands on a heavy gold-headed cane. He
wore the ordinary European dress of the
time, but there was an elaborate neatness, a
studied refinement in his appearance singular enough amidst the rude settlers of the
New World. His ruffles were made of
the finest lace, and the buckles on his
shoes silver gilt. There was nothing the
least remarkable in the face or attitude of
this stranger, nothing that would have attracted attention at Paris or perhaps at New
Orleans; but it was out of keeping with the
rough activity of the men and the wild
character of the scenery in that remote
region. His pale grey eyes, shaded with
white eyebrows, wandered listlessly over the
busy scene, and he gave a nervous start
whenever a tree fell with a louder crash
than usual. One of the labourers had left
an axe on the grass near where he was
standing. He raised it as if to measure its
weight, but his feeble grasp could not retain
its hold of the heavy implement, and it fell
to the ground. D'Auban stepped forward
to pick it up and restore it to him. He
thanked him, and said in French, but with a

German accent, that he would not meddle with it any more. This little incident served as an introduction, and the old man seemed pleased to find somebody not too busy to talk to him. His own observations betrayed great ignorance as to the nature of the country or the general habits of colonists. He talked about the want of accommodation he had met with in America, and the dirty state of the Indian villages, as if he had been travelling through a civilised country. He told d'Auban that he intended to purchase land in that neighbourhood, and to build a house.

'I begin to despair,' he said, 'of finding one which would suit us to buy or to hire. I suppose, sir, you do not know of one?'

'Certainly not of one to let,' d'Auban answered with a smile, for the idea of hiring a house in the backwoods struck him in a ludicrous light.

'But I have had a concession left on my hands by a friend who has returned to Europe, and which has upon it a house very superior to anything we see in this part of the world. Many thousand francs have been spent on this little pavillon, which is reckoned quite a curiosity, and goes by the name of the Vicomte de Harlay's Folly. The purchaser of the concession would get the house simply thrown into the bargain.'

'That sounds very well,' exclaimed the old man ; 'I think it would suit us.'

'Well, M. de Harlay has empowered me to dispose of his land and house. It is close to my own plantation, a few leagues up the river. I should be very happy to let you see it, and to explain its advantages as an investment. I am going back there this morning, and if you would like to visit it at once, I am quite at your orders. We have still the day before us.'

The stranger bowed, coughed, and then said in a hesitating manner—

' Am I by any chance speaking to Colonel d'Auban ? '

' Yes, I am Colonel d'Auban, *pour vous servir*, as the peasants say in France.'

' Then indeed, sir, I am inexpressibly honoured and delighted to have made your acquaintance. I have been assured that in this country an honest man is a rarity which Diogenes might well have needed his lanthorn to discover. A merchant at New Orleans, to whom I brought letters of introduction, told me that if I was going to the Illinois I should try to consult Colonel d'Auban about the purchase of a plantation, and not hesitate a moment about following his advice. I therefore gratefully accept your obliging proposal. but I must beg you to be so good as to allow me first to inform my daughter of our intended excursion. I will be with you again in a quarter of an hour, my amiable friend, ready and happy to surrender myself to your invaluable guidance.'

'Who is that gentleman?' asked d'Auban of the German overseer, as soon as the little old man had trotted away.

'He is called M. de Chambelle. Though his name is French, I think he is a German. Nobody knows whence he comes, or why he is come at all. He talks of houses and gardens, as if he was living in France or in Saxony. I wish him joy of the villas he will find here. And then he speaks to the Indians and the negroes for all the world as if they were Christians.'

'Many of them are Christians, M. Klein,

and often better ones than ourselves,' observed d'Auban.

'Oh! I did not mean Christians in that sense. It is only a way of speaking, you know.'

'True,' said d'Auban. 'A man told me the other day, that his horse was so clever that he never forgave or forgot—just like a Christian.'

The overseer laughed.

'You should see that old gentleman bowing and speechifying to the Indian women. He said the other day to a hideous old squaw, "*Madame la Sauvagesse*, will you sell me some of the fruit your fair hands have gathered?" She said she would give him some *without intention*, which in their phraseology means without expecting to be paid. The next day, however, she came to his hut, and enquired if he was not going to give *her* something *without intention*. The poor old man, who is dreadfully afraid of the natives, was obliged to part with some clothes Madame la Sauvagesse had taken a fancy to.'

'Has M. de Chambelle a daughter?'

'Yes, a pale handsome woman, much too

delicate and helpless, from what I hear, for this sort of hand-to-mouth life. They say she is a widow. It is somewhat funny that the French people who come here almost always stick a *de* before their names. The father is called M. *de* Chambelle, and the daughter, Madame *de* Moldau.'

'Do you know if they have brought letters of introduction with them to anyone in this or the neighbouring settlements?'

'I have not heard that they have; except M. Koli and yourself, there is scarcely a planter hereabouts whom it would be of any advantage to know.'

'I thought as they were Germans that some of your countrymen might have written about them.'

'We are a poor set here now that M. Law's grand schemes have come to nought. We do a little business on our own account by felling and selling trees, and it is lucky we do so, for not a sou of his money have we seen for a long time. It is impossible to maintain his slaves, and the plantation is going to ruin. Ah! there is M. de Chambelle coming back; did you ever see such a figure for an *habitant*?   One would fancy he carried a hair-dresser about, his hair is always so neatly powdered.'

'Will a long walk tire you?' asked d'Auban as his new acquaintance joined them, ' or will you ride my horse ? Do not have any scruples. No amount of walking ever tires me.'

' Dear sir, if we might both walk I should like it better,' answered M. de Chambelle, glancing uneasily at the horse, who, weary of the long delay, was pawing in a manner he did not quite fancy. 'If you will now and then lend me your arm, I can keep on my legs without fatigue for three or four hours.'

D'Auban passed the horse's bridle over his arm, and led the way to an opening in the forest, through which they had to pass on their way to the Pavillon St. Agathe, which was the proper name of M. de Harlay's *habitation*. Whenever they came to a rough bit of ground he gave his arm to his companion, who leant upon it lightly, and chatted as he went along with a sort of child-like confidence in his new friend.   D'Auban's concession, and the neighbouring one of St.

Agathe, were situated much higher up the river than the German settlement. His own house was close to the water-side. The pavillon stood on an eminence in the midst of a beautiful grove, and overlooked a wide extent of prairie land, bounded only in one direction by the outline of the Rocky Mountains. The magnificent scenery which surrounded this little oasis, the luxuriant vegetation, the grandeur of the wide spreading trees, the domes of blossom which here and there showed amidst masses of verdure, the numberless islets scattered over the surface of the broad-bosomed river, the shady recesses and verdant glades which formed natural alleys and bowers in its encircling forest, combined to make its position so beautiful, that it almost accounted for M. de Harlay's short-lived but violent fancy for his transatlantic property. It was a lovely scene which met the eyes of the pedestrians, when about mid-day they reached the brow of the hill. A noontide stillness reigned in the savannahs, where herds of buffaloes reposed in the long grass. Now and then a slight tremulous motion, like a ripple on the sea, stirred that boundless expanse of green, but not a sound of human or animal life rose from its flowery depths.

Not so in the grove round the pavillon. There the ear was almost deafened by the multifarious cries of beasts, the chirpings of birds, the hum of myriads of insects. The eye was dazzled by the rapidity of their movements. Hares and rabbits and squirrels darted every instant out of the thickets, and monkeys grinned and chattered amongst the branches. Winged creatures of every shape and hue were springing out of the willow grass, hovering over clusters of roses, swinging on the cordages of the grape vine, flying up into the sky, diving in the streamlets, fluttering amongst the leaves, and producing a confused murmur very strange to an unaccustomed ear.

Neither the magnificence of the scenery nor the vivacity of the denizens of the surrounding grove attracted much of M. de Chambelle's attention. When he caught sight of the pavillon, he burst forth in exclamations of delight. 'Is it possible!' he exclaimed. 'Do I really see, not a cabin or a hut, not one

of those abominable wigwams, but a house,
a real house! fit for civilised people to live
in! and is it really to be sold, my dear
sir, there, just as it stands, furniture, birds,
flowers, and all?   What may be the price of
this charming *habitation?*'

D'Auban named the sum he thought it fair
to ask for the plantation, and said the house
was included in the purchase.   M. de Chambelle took out his pocket-book and made a
brief calculation.

'It will do perfectly well,' he exclaimed.
'The interest of this sum will not exceed the
rent we should have had to pay for a house
at New Orleans.   It is exactly what we
wanted.'

'You have been fortunate to hit upon it,
then,' said d'Auban with a smile, 'for I
suppose that from the mouth of the Mississippi
to the sources of the Missouri you would not
have found such a habitation as my poor
friend's Folly.   However, as Providence has
conducted you to this spot, and you think the
établissement will suit you, we better go over
the house and afterwards visit the plantations,
in order that you may judge of the present

condition and the prospects of the concession.'

'I do not much care about that, my dear
sir. My knowledge on agricultural subjects
is very limited, and I am no judge of crops.
Indeed I greatly doubt if I should know a
field of maize from one of barley, or distinguish between a coffee, and a cotton
plantation.'

D'Auban looked in astonishment at his
companion. 'Is this a cunning adventurer,
or the most simple of men?' was the thought
in his mind as he led M. de Chambelle into
the house, who was at once as much delighted
with the inside as he had been with the outside of the building. The entrance-chamber
was decorated with the skins of various wild
animals, and the horns of antelopes ingeniously
arranged in the form of trophies. Bows and
arrows, hatchets, tomahawks, and clubs, all
instruments of Indian warfare, were hanging
against the walls. There was a small room
on one side of this hall fitted up with exquisite
specimens of Canadian workmanship, and pos-
sessing several articles of European furniture,
which had been conveyed at an immense

expense from New Orleans. There was an appearance of civilisation, if not of what we should call comfort, in this parlour, as well as in two sleeping chambers, in which real beds were to be found; a verandah, which formed a charming sitting-room in hot weather, and at the back of the house a well-fitted up kitchen, put the finishing touch to M. de Chambelle's ecstasies.

'One could really fancy oneself in Europe,' he exclaimed, rubbing his hands with delight.

'I do not think Madame de Moldan will believe her eyes when she sees this charming pavillon. It is really more than we could have expected. . . .'

'I should think so, indeed,' said d'Auban, laughing. 'You might have travelled far and wide before you stumbled on such a house in the New World.'

'Ah, the New World—the New World, my dear sir. Don't you find it dreadfully uncivilised? I cannot accustom myself to the manners of the savages. Their counte-nances are so wild, their habits so unpleasant, there is something so—so, in short, so savage in all their ways, that I cannot feel at all at home with them. By-the-bye, there is only one thing I do not like in this delightful *habitation*.'

'What is it?'

I am afraid it is a very solitary residence. You see the Indian servant, our negro boy, Madame de Moldau, and myself, we do not compose a very formidable garrison.'

'But my house is at a stone's throw from this one. In the winter you can see it through those trees, and then the wigwams of our labourers are scattered about at no great distance.'

'Ah, your labourers live in wigwams! Horrible things, I think ; but I suppose they are used to them. Have you many savages, then, in your employment ?'

'I have some Indian labourers, but they are Christians, and no longer deserve the name of savages. I like them better than the negroes. My French servants and I live in the house I spoke of.'

'Oh, then it is all right, all charming, all perfect. With a loud cry of "A moi, mes amis, Messieurs les Sauvages are upon us!" we could call you to our assistance. Well, my dear sir, I wish to conclude the purchase of this place as soon as possible. Will it suit your convenience if I give you a cheque on Messrs. Dumont et Compagnie, New Orleans?'

'Certainly. I have no doubt they will undertake to transmit the amount to M. de Harlay's bankers in Paris.'

'I hope we may be allowed to take possession of the house without much delay. Madame de Moldau is so weary of the vile hut where we have spent so many weeks.'

'I can take upon myself to place the pavillon at once at your disposal for a few days, and you can then make up your mind at leisure about concluding the purchase.'

'Thank you, my dear sir; but my mind is, I assure you, quite made up. I am sure we could go farther and fare worse; the saying was never more applicable.'

'But you are not at all acquainted yet with the state or the value of the concession. You have not gone over the accounts of the last years.'

'Is that necessary?'

'Indispensable, I should say,' d'Auban answered, rather coldly.

'It would be quite impossible, I suppose, to let us have the house without the land? You see it will suit us perfectly as a residence, but I do not see how I am to manage the business of the concession. Is not that what you call it?'

D'Auban, more puzzled than ever by the simplicity of this avowal, exclaimed, 'But in the name of patience, sir, what can you want a house for in this country, unless you intend to work the land? You do not mean, I suppose, to throw it out of cultivation and to sell the slaves?'

'O no! I suppose that would not be right. There are slaves, too. I had not thought of that. Who has managed it all since M. de Harlay went away?'

'I have.'

'Then you will help me with your advice?' This idea made M. de Chambelle brighten up like a person who suddenly sees a ray of light in a dark wood. 'Oh yes, of course, everything must go on as usual, and you will put me in the way of it all.'

'I now propose,' said d'Auban, 'that we take some refreshment at my house, where you can see the accounts, and then that we should go over the plantations.'

'By all means, by all means,' cried M. de Chambelle, trying to put a good face on the matter. 'And as we walk along, you can point out the principal things that have to be attended to in the management of a concession.'

During the remainder of the day, d'Auban took great pains to explain to his guest the nature and capabilities of his proposed purchase, and the amount of its value as an investment. M. de Chambelle listened with great attention, and assented to everything. Two or three times he interrupted him with such remarks as these: 'She will like the low couch in the parlour;' or 'Madame de Moldau can sit in the verandah on fine summer evenings;' or again, 'I hope the noise of the birds and insects will not annoy Madame de Moldau. Do you think, my dear sir, the slaves could drive them away?'

'I am afraid that would be a task beyond their power,' d'Auban said as gravely as he

could. But depend upon it, after the first few
days your daughter will get so accustomed
to the sound as scarcely to hear it. I am
afraid,' he added, 'she must have suffered
very much during the voyage up the river?'

'Oh yes, she has suffered very much,' the
old man answered ; and then he hastened to
change the subject by asking some question
about crops, which certainly evinced an
incredible absence of the most ordinary
knowledge and experience in such matters.

Before they parted, M. de Chambelle and
d'Auban agreed that in the afternoon of the
following day he should remove with his
daughter to St. Agathe. D'Auban offered to
fetch them himself in his boat and to send a
barge for their luggage. M. de Chambelle
thanked him very much, hesitated a little,
and then said that, if he would not take it
amiss, he should beg of him not to come
himself, but only to send his boatmen.
Madame de Moldau was so unaccustomed
to the sight of strangers, and in such delicate
health, that the very efforts she would make
to express her gratitude to Colonel d'Auban
would tax her strength too severely. He felt

a little disappointed, but of course assented. The following morning he went through the rooms of the pavillon, arranging and re-arranging the furniture, and conveying from his own house some of the not over-abundant articles it contained to the chamber Madame de Moldau was to occupy.

'Antoine,' he said to his servant, who was in the kitchen at St. Agathe, storing it with provisions, 'just go home and fetch me the two pictures in my study; the walls here look so bare.'

'But Monsieur's own room will look very dull without them,' answered Antoine, who by no means approved of the dismantling process which had been going on all the morning in his master's house.'

'Never mind, I want them here; and bring some nails and some string with you.'

A little water-colour view of a castle on a cliff and a tolerable copy of the Madonna della Seggiola soon ornamented the lady's bed-room, whilst a selection from his scanty library gave a home-like appearance to the little parlour. A basket full of grapes was placed on the table, and then Thérèse came in with an immense nosegay in her hand.

'Ah! that is just what I wanted,' d'Auban exclaimed.

'For the nest of the white dove,' she answered, with the sudden lighting up of the eye which supplies the place of a smile in an Indian face.

'You see we have found a cage for your wounded bird, Thérèse, and now we shall have to tame her.'

'Ah!' cried Thérèse, putting her hand to her mouth—a token of admiration amongst the Indians—'you have brought her pictures, which will not fade like my poor flowers.'

'But she may get tired of the pictures, and you may bring her, if you like, fresh flowers every day.'

'Look,' said Thérèse, pointing to the river. 'There is your boat; they are coming.'

'So they are. I did not expect them so soon.'

He sent Antoine to meet the strangers and conduct them to the house, and walked across the wooded lawn to his own home. All the evening he felt unsettled. In his monotonous life an event of any sort was an unusual excitement. He went in and out of the house, paced restlessly up and down the margin of the stream. His eyes were continually turning towards the pavillon, from the chimney of which, for the first time for three years, smoke was issuing. He watched that blue curling smoke, and felt as if it warmed his heart. Perhaps he had suffered from a sense of loneliness more than he was quite aware of, and that the thought of those helpless beings close at hand, of whom he knew so little, but who inspired him with a vague interest, was an unconscious relief. He pictured them to himself in their new home. He wondered what impression the first sight of it had made on Madame de Moldau, and then he tried to fancy what she was like. Thérèse thought her beautiful, and the German overseer said she was handsome. She was not, in that case, like her father. Would he feel disappointed when he saw her? Would she turn out to be a good-looking woman with white cheeks and yellow hair, such as an Indian and a German boor would admire, one because it was the first of the sort she had seen, and the other because he had not known any others. He missed his pictures a little. The room, as Antoine had said, would look dull without them. Perhaps they had not attracted her notice at all, or if they had, she did not perhaps care at all about them. He grew tired of thinking, but could not banish the subject from his mind. As the shades of evening deepened, and the crescent moon arose, and myriads of stars, 'the common people of the sky,' as Sir Henry Wootton calls them, showed one by one in the blue vault of heaven, and were pictured in the mirror of the smooth broad river, he still wandered about the grove, whence he could see St. Agathe and the window of the chamber which he supposed was Madame de Moldau's. There was a light in it—perhaps she was reading one of his books—perhaps she was gazing on the dark woods and shining river, and thinking of a far-distant home. She was weeping, perhaps, or praying, or sleeping. 'Again,' he impatiently exclaimed, 'again at this guessing work! What a fool I am! What are these people to me, and why on earth have they come here?'

That last question he was destined very often to put to himself, with more or less of curiosity, of anxiety, and it might be, of pain, as time went on.

The purchaser of St. Agathe was enchanted with his new possession, and began in earnest, as he considered, to apply himself to his new pursuits as an agriculturist and planter, but the absurd mistakes which attended his first attempts at the management of his property, increased d'Auban's astonishment that a man so unfitted for business should ever have thought of becoming a settler. Instruction and advice were simply thrown away on M. de Chambelle. He might as well have talked to a child about the management of a plantation, and he plainly foresaw that unless some more experienced person were entrusted with the business, the concession might be as well at once given up. At the end of a few days he frankly told him as much, and advised him to engage some other emigrant to act as his agent, or to join him as a partner in the speculation.

M. de Chambelle eagerly caught at the idea, and proposed to d'Auban himself to enter into partnership with him.

'Indeed, my dear Colonel,' he urged, 'you will be doing a truly charitable action. Whom else could I trust? on whose honour could I rely in this dreadful country of savages and settlers, many of whom have not more conscience than the natives?'

'Not half as much, I fear,' said d'Auban; 'but you could write to M. Dumont and ask him to look out for you at New Orleans——'

'And in the meantime ruin the plantation and go out of my mind. M. d'Auban, do consider my position.'

There was an eager wistful expression on the old man's face, which at once touched and provoked d'Auban, and 'why on earth did he put himself in that position?' was his inward exclamation. He was not in a very good humour that day. He could not help feeling a little hurt at the manner in which, whilst he was assisting her father in every possible way, and showering kindnesses upon them, Madame de Moldau avoided him. M. de Chambelle had asked him one day to call at St. Agathe, and assured him that, much as she dreaded the sight of strangers, she really did wish to make his acquaintance. D'Auban said he would go with him to the pavillon, but begged him to wait a few minutes till he had finished directing some letters which a traveller was going to take with him that evening. M. de Chambelle sat down, and as each letter was thrown on the table, he read the directions. One of them was to a Prince Mitroski, at St. Petersburg. As they were walking to St. Agathe, he asked d'Auban if he had ever been in Russia.

'Yes,' was the answer. 'I was there for some years.'

'How long ago, my dear sir?'

'I left it about five years ago.'

'Were you in the Russian service?'

'Yes, I commanded a regiment of artillery. And you, M. de Chambelle, have you ever been at St. Petersburg?'

'Oh, I have been all over the world,' M. de Chambelle answered with a shrug, and then began to chatter in his random sort of way, passing from one subject to another without allowing time for any comments. When they arrived at the pavillon, he begged d'Auban to wait in the parlour, and went to look for Madame de Moldau.

In a few minutes he returned, and said she
had a bad headache, and begged M. d'Auban
to excuse her. Several days had elapsed
since then, and no message had been sent to
invite his return. He felt a little angry with
the lady, and still more with himself, for
caring whether she saw him or not.

Foolish as all this was, it did not incline
him to a favourable consideration of M. de
Chambelle's proposal.

'You are so clever,' the latter pleaded. 'You
know all about this concession, and you manage
your own so beautifully, and you understand
so well how to behave to the labourers.
When I speak civilly to them they laugh, and
if I find fault they turn their backs upon me,
and make remarks in their own language,
which I have every reason to suppose are not
over and above polite. We are not in any
particular hurry about profits; I do not
mind letting you into the secret. We have
got a large sum of money at the banker's at
New Orleans, and I can draw upon them if
necessary. You would then make all the
bargains for us with Messieurs les Sauvages,
and I need not have anything to say to them.

I cannot tell you how happy it would make me, and Madame de Moldau also.'

'Indeed!' d'Auban said, with a rather scornful smile.

'Of course you would make your own conditions. I assure you that I look upon it as a providential event to have met with such a friend as you have been to us in this land of savages and alligators. By the way, I forgot to tell you how narrowly I escaped yesterday one of those horrible animals.'

' Your reliance on Providence seems to me to have been carried to excess,' d'Auban observed, still in a sarcastic tone. 'Suppose we had not met, what would you have done? Your daughter could not have endured the ordinary hardships of a settler's life. Had it not been for St. Agathe——'

' Aye, and for Colonel d'Auban, what would have become of us? But you see she would come to Louisiana, and when we got to New Orleans nothing would serve her but to come on to this place. What could I do?'

D'Auban laughed. ' Is it, then, the new fashion in France for parents to obey their children?

'Ah! ce que femme veut Dieu le veut! One cannot refuse her anything.'

'Perhaps she has had some great sorrow. Has she lost her husband lately?'

'I suppose she has suffered everything a woman can suffer,' the old man answered, in a tone of feeling which touched d'Auban.

'She has one great blessing left,' he kindly said—'an affectionate father.'

'O no, no! what can such a one as I do for her? But what I meant was that if she is bent upon a thing——'

'She cannot be dissuaded from it,' said d'Auban, again smiling.

'Well, I could never say nay to a lady, and when you see Madame de Moldau——'

'I shall understand that her wishes are not to be resisted. I am quite willing to believe it.'

'But with regard to the partnership, M. d'Auban.'

'Well, I am sure you will excuse my speaking plainly, M. de Chambelle. I perfectly admit that you cannot manage your property yourself, but at the same time I would greatly prefer your applying to some other colonist to join you in the undertaking.'

' What is the use of talking to me of some other colonist? Is there a single person in this neighbourhood whom you could now really recommend to me as a partner? Only consider how I am situated.'

' Et que diable est-il venu faire dans cette galère !' muttered d'Auban, and then said out loud : ' But it is impossible to conclude an arrangement of this kind in an off-hand manner. There must be an agreement drawn up and signed before witnesses.'

' By all means, my dear sir, as many as you please.'

' But such formalities are not easily accomplished in a place like this.'

' Then, for heaven's sake, let us dispense with them ! The case lies in a nut-shell. I have purchased this land for the sake of the little bijou of a house upon it ; and as regards the plantation, I am much in the same position as a Milord Anglais I once heard of, who bought Polichinelle, and was surprised to find, when he brought it home, that it did not act of its own accord. I have used my best endeavours to master the subject. I have tried to assume the manners

of a planter; but *chassez le naturel, il re-
vient au galop*, and mine is cantering back
as fast as possible to its starting-point. There
are things a man can do, and others he can't.
I was not made for a colonist.'

D'Auban was very near saying, 'What
were you made for?' but he checked the
sneering thought. In the prime of life and
full enjoyment of a vigorous intellect, he had
been tempted to despise the feeble fidgetty
old man before him, forgetting that the race
is not always to the swift or the battle to the
strong. We sometimes wonder what part
some particular person is sent to fulfill on
earth. He or she seems to our short-sighted
view so insignificant, so incapable, so devoid
of the qualities we most admire, and all the
while, perhaps, what appears to us his or her
deficiencies, are qualifications for the task or
the position assigned to them by Providence.
There are uses for timid spirits, weak frames,
and broken hearts, little dreamed of by those
who, in the pride of health and mental vigour,
know little of their value.

Some further conversation took place between the neighbours, which ended by
d'Auban's promising to draw up an agreement

based on M. de Chambelle's proposal. It was further decided that they would take this paper to the Mission of St. Francis, and request Father Maret and another French *habitant* to witness its signature. A day or two afterwards this was accordingly done. M. de Chambelle rubbed his hands in a transport of delight, and complimented Father Maret on the beauty of his church, in which he had never set his foot, The missionary was amused at hearing himself called M. l'Abbé, and took an opportunity, whilst his guest was flitting about his rose-bushes like a superannuated butterfly, to ask d'Auban for the history of his new partner.

'I am almost ashamed to own how little I know of him,' was his answer. And then he gave a brief account of the arrival of these strangers — of the purchase of St. Agathe, and M. de Chambelle's total inability to manage the concession. When Father Maret had heard the particulars, he smiled and said, ' This partnership is, then, an act of charity. But take care, my dear friend, how you involve yourself with these people. I strongly advise you to be prudent. We have hitherto been rather out of the reach of adventurers, but there seems to me something a little suspicious in the apparent helplessness of this gentleman. Do not let pity or kindness throw you off your guard.'

'If he were to turn out a rogue, which I hardly can believe possible, he could not do me any harm. You see he leaves everything in my hands. I might cheat him, but he cannot injure me. I shall feel to understand him better when I have seen his daughter. Is it not strange her shutting herself up so entirely?'

'There seems to me something strange about the whole affair. Have you sent his cheque to New Orleans?'

'Yes, and took the opportunity of asking M. Dumont what he knew about him; but months may elapse, as you know, before I get an answer.'

'The daughter is, to my mind, the most doubtful feature in the case. It is not often that European women of good character come out to the colonies. Who knows what this one may be? It is not impossible that all this hiding is only a trick by which she hopes to pique your curiosity, and interest your feelings. But here comes your friend. Poor old man! He certainly does not look like an impostor.'

The partners took their leave. As they walked away, it was impossible not to be struck by the contrast presented by d'Auban's tall figure and firm step, and his companion's ungraceful form and shuffling gait, or to see the latter's admiring confiding manner towards his companion and doubt its sincerity. The priest could not, however, divest himself of a vague apprehension as to the character and designs of the strangers. Experience had taught him sad lessons with regard to colonial speculators, and his fatherly affection for d'Auban made him suspicious of their designs. It was in Russia that the intimacy between these two men had begun, and in America it had deepened into friendship. There was a difference of at least twenty years between their ages. Father Maret was bent with toil, and his countenance bore the traces of a life of labour and privations. When at rest, melancholy was its characteristic expression, as if continual contact with sin and sorrow had left its impress upon it; but when he conversed with others, it was with a bright and gracious smile. His step, though heavy, was rapid, as that of a man who, weary and exhausted, yet hastens on in the service of God. His head fell slightly forward on his breast, and his hair was thin and grey, but in his eye there was a fire, and in his manner and language an energy which did not betoken decay of body or mind.

The first years he had spent in America had been very trying. Till d'Auban's arrival he had seldom been cheered by intercourse with those who could share in his interests or his anxieties, or afford him the mental relief which every educated person finds in the society of educated men. Some of the Indian Christians were models of piety and full of childlike faith and amiability; but there must always exist an intellectual gulph between minds untrained and uncultivated and those which have been used from childhood upward to live almost as much in the past as in the present; and this is even the

case to a certain degree as regards religion.
The advantage in this respect may not always
be on the side of civilisation and of a high
amount of mental culture. There is often
in persons wise unto salvation and ignorant
of all else, a simplicity of faith, a clear real-
isation of its great truths and unhesitating
acceptance of its teachings, which may very
well excite admiration and something like
envy in those whom an imperfect, and therefore deceptive, knowledge misleads, and who
are sometimes almost weary of the multipli-
city of their own thoughts. But it is nevertheless impossible that they should not miss,
in their intercourse with others, the power of
association which links their religious belief
with a whole chain of reminiscences, and con-
nects it with a number of outlying regions
bordering on its domain. Viewed in the
light of faith, art, science, literature, history,
politics, every achievement of genius, every
past and present event, every invention, every
discovery, has a peculiar significancy. Names
become beacons in the stream of time—signal
lights, bright or lurid as may be, which the
lapse of ages never extinguishes. This con-

tinued train of thought, this kingdom of association, this region of sympathy, is the growth of centuries, and to forego familiarity with it one of the greatest sacrifices which a person of intellectual habits can make. D'Auban's society and friendship had filled up this void in Father Maret's existence, and there was another far greater trial which his residence in this settlement had tended to mitigate.

In New France, as in all recently-discovered countries, a missionary's chief difficulty consisted not in converting the natives, or (a greater one) in keeping them from relapsing into witchcraft and idolatry—not in the wearisome pursuit of his scattered sheep over morasses, sluggish streams, and dreary savannahs—but in the bad example set by the European settlers. It was the hardened irreligion, the scoffing spirit, the profligate lives of the emigrants swarming on the banks of the Mississippi, tainting and polluting the forests and prairies of this new Eden with their vile passions and remorseless thirst for gold, which wrung the heart of the Christian priest, and brought a blush to his cheek when the Indians asked—'Are the white men Christians? Do they worship Jesus?'

He felt sometimes inclined to answer, 'No; their god is mammon, a very hateful idol.' To make his meaning clear, he used to show them a piece of gold, and to say that for the sake of that metal many a baptised European imperilled his immortal soul. The Indians of the Mission got into the habit of calling gold the white man's manitou, that is, his domestic idol. It became, therefore, an immense consolation to Father Maret when a Frenchman came into the neighbourhood whom he could point out to the native converts as an example of the practical results of true religion. He was wont to say that d'Auban's goodness and Thérèse's virtues made more converts than his sermons. His own example he, of course, counted for nothing. It was not, then, extraordinary that he should feel anxious about the character of the new inhabitants of St. Agathe, and their probable intimacy with his friend. He had often regretted that one so well fitted for domestic life and social enjoyments should be cut off by circumstances from congenial society. The amount of friendly intercourse which was amply sufficient for his own need of relaxation could not be so for one whose solitary existence was an accident, not a vocation. He might not be conscious of it as yet, but with advancing years the want of a home and of friends was sure to be more keenly felt. Glad, indeed, would he have been to think that this partnership, that these new acquaintances, were likely to fill up this void, and to prove a blessing to his friend. Never was a more fervent prayer breathed for another's weal than that which rose from Father Maret's heart that night for the companion of his solitude. None feel more solicitude for the happiness, or more sympathy with the trials of others, than those who have renounced earthly happiness themselves. There is something in their sympathy akin to a mother's love or a guardian angel's pity.

Thérèse met the priest as he was turning back towards the village. After saluting him in the Indian fashion, she said, 'The eagle spreads his wings over the nest of the white dove. The strong befriends the weak. It is good, my father.'

'I hope so,' the black robe kindly answered, as he led the way into the church, where the people were assembling for evening prayer.

CHAPTER III.

The present hour repeats upon its strings
  Echoes of some vague dream we have forgot;
Dim voices whisper half-remembered things,
  And when we pause to listen—answer not.

Forebodings come, we know not how or whence,
  Shadowing a nameless fear upon the soul,
And stir within our hearts a subtler sense
  Than light may read, or wisdom may control.

And who can tell what secret links of thought
  Bind heart to heart? Unspoken things are heard,
As if within our deepest selves was brought
  The soul, perhaps, of some unuttered word.
                      Adelaide Proctor.

M. DE CHAMBELLE, no longer the manager of a concession, trod the earth with a lighter step, and strolled through the plantations, bowing affably to the negroes and chatting with those of the labourers who spoke French or German. As to d'Auban, he applied himself to the business he had undertaken with his usual energy and intelligence—an additional amount of labour was a boon to him. He had 'the frame of adamant and soul of fire,' to which work is as necessary as food or air. He was glad also to adopt, with regard to the slaves on the St. Agathe estate, the measures he had successfully carried out for the benefit of his own labourers. Though he had not yet seen Madame de Moldau, the very thought of a European lady such as Thérèse had described her living so near him, in the house he used to call a folly, seemed to make a difference in his life. At all hours of the day he pictured her to himself, and tried to imagine her existence within those four walls, with no other companion than her garrulous old father, who chattered as if he could keep nothing to himself, and yet never dropped a word that threw light on her sorrow or her story, whatever it was, or gave the least clue to their past history.

One evening, as he was passing through the shubbery, he caught sight of her on the balcony of the pavillon. Her head was thrown back as if to catch the breeze just beginning to rise at the close of a sultry day.

He stood riveted to the spot. 'She is very beautiful,' he said, half aloud, 'much more beautiful than I expected.' She turned her head and their eyes met, which made him start and instantly draw back. He was distressed at having been surprised gazing at her, but he could not help feeling glad he had seen her at last. Who was she like? Very like somebody he had seen before, but he could not remember where. 'I am sure her face is not a new one to me,' he thought. 'How intensely blue her eyes are! What a very peculiar-looking person she is! Her dress is different, too, from anything we see here. What was it? A black silk gown, I think, opening in front, and a lace cap fastened on each side with coral pins. What a start she gave when she saw me! I am so sorry I took her by surprise. I ought of all things to have avoided the appearance of a rude vulgar curiosity.' That self-reproach occupied him all the evening. He made it an excuse to himself for thinking of nothing but Madame de Moldau. He was at once excited and depressed. All sorts of fancies, some sad and some pleasant, passed through his mind. Europe with all his associations rose before him, conjured up by the sight of that pale woman dressed in black.

For the first time since leaving France a vague yearning, half regret, half presentiment, filled his heart. Can we doubt that there are such things as presentiments? True, we are sometimes haunted by a besetting thought, or we have an agitating dream, or we are seized by an unaccountable depression which we consider as a foreboding of coming evil, of some event which, in the poet's words, casts its shadows before it, and the thought passes away, the dream fades in the light of morning, a draught of spring's delicious air or a ray of genial sunshine dispels the melancholy which a moment before seemed incurable, and the voice which rang in our ear like a warning, subsides amidst the busy sounds of life, leaving no echo behind it. True, this frequently happens, and yet in spite of these deceptions, we cannot altogether disbelieve in the occasional occurrence of subtle and mysterious intimations which forebade future events, and, like whispers from heaven, prepare our souls for coming joys or sorrows.

Was it an effect of memory, or a trick of the imagination, or a simple delusion, which played the fool that night with d'Auban's well-regulated mind, suggesting to him a fantastic resemblance between the face he had seen that evening and a vision of his earlier years? Was it a presentiment of happiness or a warning of evil which stirred the calm depths of his tranquil soul, as he mused on days gone by? He did not know; he did not analyse his feelings, but gave himself up to a long reverie, in which, like in a drowning man's dream, the events of his life passed successively before him with a strange distinctness. How the remembrance of our childhood comes back to us as we advance in life! We lose sight of it amidst the noise and excitement of youth and middle age; but when the shades of evening fall, and the busy hum of voices subsides, and silence steals on the soul as it spreads over a darkening landscape, the thought returns of what we were when we started on that long journey now drawing to a close. And even in the noon-tide of life there are seasons when we pause and look back as d'Auban did that night. When the future assumes a new aspect, and we dimly foresee a change in our destiny, without discerning its form, even as a blind man is conscious of approach to an object he does not yet touch or behold, a feeling of this sort sometimes drives us back upon the past, as to a friend left behind, and well-nigh lost sight of.

On the following evening to the one when d'Auban had for the first time seen Madame de Moldau, her father walked into his room and in a tone of unusual importance and animation invited him to dinner for the next day. The blood mounted into d'Auban's face. He longed to accept, but pride disinclined him to do so. After the great reluctance she had evinced to see him, he did not like to thrust himself into her society by availing himself of an invitation which only gratitude or civility had, in all probability, induced her to send. He accordingly made some not very intelligible excuse.

'Ah! my dear friend,' exclaimed M. de Chambelle, 'you must not refuse; it is impossible you can refuse.'

It was with a pained expression of countenance that this remonstrance was made. The old man seemed shocked and hurt.

'Indeed, my dear sir,' said d'Auban kindly, 'my only reason for refusing is, that I fear my presence will not be acceptable to your daughter, and perhaps compel her, as she did before, to keep her own room.'

'Ah! that was because she had a headache. Of course you would not wish her to appear if she was ill.'

'Of course not. I only wish you would not consider yourself obliged to invite me; I assure you I do not expect it.'

'But she wishes to see you, and thank you for all your kindness and civility. Indeed, I cannot tell her that you refuse to come.'

'Well, if you make a point of it, I shall be happy to accept your kind invitation. At what o'clock do you dine?'

'At one,' answered M. de Chambelle; and then recovering his spirits he added, 'Our *cuisine*, I am sorry to say, is of the New World school, in spite of all my efforts to instruct our Indian vatel in the mysteries of French cooking; but having witnessed the hermit-like nature of your repasts, I am not afraid of your despising the roasted kid and wild ducks which the female savage has provided for our entertainment. We will add to it a little glass of " essence of fire," as the Indians call our good French cognac. Well, I will not take up your time now. To-morrow at one o'clock; you will not forget.'

When he had reached the door, M. de Chambelle turned back again, and, laying his hand on d'Auban's arm, he said in a tremulous voice :

'You will not be angry if she should change her mind and not appear to-morrow? Her spirits are very unequal ; you don't know what she has gone through.'

He was a poor creature enough this old M. de Chambelle, and d'Auban had difficulty sometimes in not despising the weakness and frivolity he evinced in the midst of troubles, into which he had so recklessly plunged himself; but he never heard him speak of his daughter without noticing a kind of pathos in his voice and manner, which redeemed in his eyes his childishness and folly, and softened his feelings towards him. He assured him that he would not take anything amiss, and promised to be punctual at the appointed time. And so he was; and on his way to St. Agathe he kept inwardly re-proaching and laughing at himself for the timidity he felt at the thought of being introduced to Madame de Moldau, and at the fear he had that after all she would not appear. When he came in sight of the pretty fanciful toy of a house, a specimen of Euro-pean refinement in the midst of the oaks and pines of an American forest, it no longer struck him as so out of place as it was wont to do when he ridiculed M. de Harlay's Folly, and blamed its erection as the idle whim of a Parisian's fancy. The woman he had seen surrounded by shining evergreens and roses in full blossom, like a lovely picture framed in flowerets, seemed a fitting inhabitant for this earthly paradise.

It had never showed to such advantage, in his eyes at least, as on this day. The brilliant foliage was shining in the full radiance of noon. The avenue of magnolias leading to the little rustic porch was fragrant with in-cense-like perfume. Not a breath stirred the branches of the encircling cedars. Beautiful birds, like winged jewels flying through the translucent air, gave life and animation to the scene, and insects lazily hovered over masses of scented woodbine, their wings weighed down with honey, and their drowsy hum lulling the ear.

M. de Chambelle was standing at the door looking out for his guest. He seemed more fidgetty still than usual as he conducted him to the room where his daughter usually sat, and then went, as he said, to inform her of his arrival. She came directly; and if d'Auban had admired her from a distance, he now did so a thousand times more. The sweetness of her countenance, the exquisite delicacy of her complexion, the pathetic expression (no other word would express it) of her large and very blue eyes, surpassed in beauty anything he could call to mind; and yet again the feeling came over him that it was not the first time he had seen that charming face, or heard that sweet voice, he mentally added, when she thanked him with a gentle dignity of manner for all he had done to make her comfortable at St. Agathe.

'It is one of the loveliest places I have ever beheld,' she said.

What touched him most was that he saw, from the quivering of her lip and the fluctuating colour of her cheek, that she was making an effort over herself in order to welcome him. Notwithstanding this visible emotion, her manner was quiet and self-possessed. He felt, on the contrary, as awkward and stupid as possible, and scarcely knew what to say in return for her acknowledgments. Man of the world as he once had been, he was quite at a loss on this occasion. She was such a different person from what he might have expected to see. At last he said, ' My friend, M. de Harlay, little imagined when he built this pavillon, or rather when he abandoned it two years ago, Madame, that it would have the good fortune to be so soon inhabited by a European lady. What in my ignorance I deemed a folly has turned out an inspiration. We emigrants are apt to build for ourselves barns or cabins rather than houses.'

' Is not your home behind those trees, M. d'Auban ? '

' Madame, it is that plain square building near the river.'

' Oh, I see it ; near those trees with the large white flowers.'

'Are you fond of flowers, Madame de Moldau?

'Could one venture to say one did not care about them?' She said this with one of those smiles which hover on the lips without in the least altering the melancholy expression of the eyes.

'In this new world, Madame,' he answered, 'may we not venture to say anything, even the truth?'

Madame de Moldau blushed, and said rather quickly, 'I find almost as much difference between one flower and another as between different persons. Some are beautiful but uninteresting, others decidedly repulsive, and some without any beauty at all are nevertheless charming. Violets, for instance, and mignonette. It has often struck me that a pretty book might be written on the characters of flowers.'

'I quite agree with you, Madame, not only about flowers, but as to all the objects which surround us. It is often difficult to tell why certain landscapes, certain animals — nay, certain faces — have a charm quite independent of beauty. It is, however, easier to discover what captivates us in a human countenance than in a landscape or a flower.'

'I suppose, sir, there are secret sympathies, mysterious affinities, between our great parent nature and ourselves which are felt, but cannot be explained ?'

'Nature is indeed a teacher, or rather a book full of instruction, but it is not every-one who has the key to its secrets.'

'I should think that in this desert you must have had many opportunities of gaining possession of this important key.'

'No doubt there are lessons broad-scattered on the surface of nature which he who runs may read, but my life here has been too busy a one for much study or thought.'

'How long, sir, have you been in this country ?'

' Five years.'

'Five years! Almost a lifetime.'

D'Auban smiled. ' That lifetime has seemed to me very short.'

'Indeed! Have you become accustomed to the monotony of this forest scenery ?'

'Not merely accustomed, but attached to it.'

'What! do you not feel oppressed by its death-like stillness? It puts me in mind of being becalmed at sea.

> Tiefe Stille herrscht im Wasser,
> Und bekümmert sieht der Fischer
> Glatte Fläche rings umher.
> Keine Luft von keiner Seite,
> Todesstille fürchterlich ;
> In die ungeheure Weite
> Reget keine Welle sich.

'Do you understand German, M. d'Auban ?'

'Not enough, Madame, to seize the sense of those lines. I have always heard that a calm at sea is more awful than a storm. And you have gone through that trial ? '

' O yes, it was horrible ; not a sound, not a breeze, not a ripple, on that smooth leaden sea for more than ten days ; and eight hundred emigrants on board a crowded vessel ! '

' Good heavens, Madame, how you must have suffered ! But does the solitude of our grand forests, teeming as they do with animal life, and full of every variety of vegetable production, affect you in the same manner ?'

' There is, I must confess, a similarity in the effect both have upon me.'

'We have sometimes winds here which play rough games with the topmost branches of our evergreen oaks.'

'Ah, well do I know it,' Madame de Moldau answered, with one of her joyless smiles. 'The very day we arrived a hurricane almost destroyed our boat. Simon was much alarmed. I suppose you know him, M. d'Auban? He says he has the honour of being acquainted with you.'

'I have long had the advantage or the disadvantage, whichever it is, of his acquaintance. He is quite a character. His boats, such as they are, prove a great convenience to emigrants; but how you, Madame de Moldau, could endure the hardships of such a voyage, I am at a loss to conceive.'

'Is there anything one cannot endure?' This was said with some bitterness. 'The voyage was bad enough,' she continued, before he had time to answer, 'but not so bad as the landing. Oh, that first night in an Indian hut! The smell, the heat, the mosquitoes, that winged army of tormentors! Is it because we are farther removed from the river that they do not assail us so much here?'

'Partly so, perhaps; but they always attack new-comers with extraordinary virulence.'

'Have you lived alone all this time, M. d'Auban?'

'M. de Harlay remained with me two years; and I often see Father Maret, the priest of the neighbouring Mission. During the hunting season I accompany him in his wanderings.'

'In search of game?'

'I pursue the game. He follows about his wandering flock in their encampments in the forests and near the great lakes.'

At that moment M. de Chambelle announced that dinner was ready. Madame de Moldan rose, and d'Auban offered to conduct her to the hall which served as a dining-room. There was a slight hesitation in her manner which caused him hastily to draw back. The colour which only occasionally visited her cheek rushed into it now. She held out her hand and lightly laid it on his. He felt it tremble, and became so confused

that he hardly knew what he was doing.
He had been accustomed to the best, which
in those days meant the most aristocratic,
society in Europe, and had often dined with
princes. How was it, then, that in that log-
built house, sitting between the old man,
whose affairs he had consented to manage
out of sheer compassion, and his young and
gentle daughter, he should feel so embarrassed?

As they sat down she pointed to a sprig
of jessamine in a nosegay on the table, and
said : 'There is a flower that has both beauty
and charm.'

'Yes,' he answered, 'and purity and sweetness also. One would not dare to deal
roughly with so delicate a flower.'

He thought there was a likeness between
that white jessamine and the woman by his
side.

She was very silent during dinner.

M. de Chambelle's eyes were always glancing towards her, and he seemed distressed at
her eating so little. Once he got up to
change her plate and offer her some other
dish than the one she had been helped to.

Before the meal was over she complained of being tired, and withdrew to the sitting-room. During the time which elapsed before she joined them, d'Auban found it very difficult to attend to his host's rambling discourse. His mind was running on the peculiarity of Madame de Moldau's manner. He could not quite satisfy himself as to the nature of this peculiarity. Nothing could be sweeter than her countenance; her voice was charming; her way of speaking courteous: but there was at the same time something a little abrupt and even slightly imperious in it. which did not take away from her attractiveness, for it was neither unfeminine or ungracious: but he could quite believe what M. de Chambelle had said, that when she was bent on anything it was not easy to oppose her. 'I suppose' (he thought) 'that she has been so idolised by her father that she takes his devotion as a matter of course, and it would indeed be extraordinary if he was not devoted to such a daughter. Had I forgotten,' he asked himself, ' what refined, well-educated women are like, or is this one very superior to what they generally are?'

When at last they left the dining-room and joined Madame de Moldau she made a sign to him to seat himself by her side, and, pointing to the view, said with a smile, ' Your beloved woods and prairies.'

' Would,' he earnestly said, ' that I might be so happy as to teach you to love them.'

She looked steadfastly before her with a fixed gaze, but it did not seem to rest on the river or on the waning foliage. Tears gathered in her eyes and rolled down her cheeks. D'Auban saw her father watching her with painful solicitude, and, not knowing how to break the silence which ensued, he turned away and looked at the books which were lying on the table. When we are for any reason interested about anyone, how eagerly we take notice of what they read, and try in this way to form some idea of their tastes and opinions! Sometimes in a railway carriage or on a bench in a public garden, we see a person absorbed in a book, and if there is anything about them which in the least excites our interest, we long to know what sort of thoughts are awakened by the volume in their hands—what feelings it touches—what emotions it excites—what amount of truth or of falsehood, of evil or good, of food or of poison, is conveyed in the pages so eagerly perused! What a wonderful thing a book is when we come to think of it! how much more we know of those we hold converse with by means of their writings than of many with whose faces we are familiar, whom we have listened to and talked to perhaps for years, without ever giving a real insight into their minds or their characters! What deep and vehement feelings have been often stirred up by the silent adversaries, the mute antagonists we encounter in the solitude of our chambers! What earnest protests we have mentally uttered when our faith has been outraged or our consciences wounded! What blessings we have showered on the writer who eloquently expresses what we ourselves have thought and felt—who defends with courage what we deem sacred and true—gives a tangible form to our vague imaginings, and raises us in his powerful grasp to the level of his own intellect! What friends of this kind we most of us have had, those at whose feet we sat when the first dawnings of intelligence threw a doubtful light on our minds—those to whom we paid an almost idolatrous worship in youth—those who have been to us fathers though they knew us not, teachers though they recked not of us, guides and comforters as life advanced, 'companions on its downward way!'

The books on Madame de Moldau's table were the 'Maxims of La Rochefoucauld,' 'Plutarch's Lives,' a volume of Corneille's Tragedies, and a German translation of the Psalms.

'Is this your travelling library, Madame de Moldau?' d'Auban asked, for the purpose of breaking a silence which was becoming awkward.

'About the whole of it, I think,' was her answer. 'It is impossible to travel with many luxuries, not even intellectual ones.'

'Would it be impertinent to ask if choice or chance influenced their selection?'

'Oh, chance decided it, like everything else in one's fate.'

'Surely you do not think that the world is governed by chance?' d'Auban exclaimed.

'I suppose I ought to have used the word providence,' Madame de Moldau answered in a careless tone.

D'Auban could not repress a sigh. 'It would be so dreadful,' he gently said, 'to suffer, and think it was the result of accident.' He had taken up the volume of German Psalms and was turning over its pages. Madame de Moldau saw it in his hands, and gave a rapid anxious look at her father, who jumped up, snatched the book from him, and, rushing to the window, pretended to kill an insect with it. 'These mosquitoes are dreadfully troublesome,' he cried. 'I really must get a net or something to hang up against this window;' and he hurried out of the room, with the volume in his hand.

'If any of my books could amuse you, Madame de Moldau,' d'Auban said, 'I should be only too happy if you would make use of my little library. I have thirty or forty volumes at my house. Nothing very new, but most of them worthy of more than one perusal.'

'You are very kind. Perhaps you will

allow me, some day, to look at them? Have you seen this volume of Corneille's Tragedies? I like them much better than Racine's.'

'I saw the Cid acted at St. Petersburg some years ago. The Czar preferred Corneille to all other dramatic writers.'

'Buffoonery and low comedy are supposed to be what he likes best, I believe.'

'I suppose that in tastes as well as in other things extremes sometimes meet. And how difficult it is to form a just estimate of that extraordinary man's character!'

'M. de Chambelle tells me you were at one time in his service. You must have admired his genius, his great qualities?'

'I admired the sovereign who, almost single-handed, changed the face of an empire, the man whose energy and perseverance effected in a few years the work of centuries; but a nearer acquaintance with this great barbarian completely changed the nature of this admiration. Wonder remained, but unaccompanied with respect. How can one respect a man who is the slave of his own passions, whose remorseless cruelty and coarse brutality are a disgrace to human nature, and who is wanting in some of its noblest attributes? The religious element does not seem to exist in him. He respects neither God nor man.'

'I have heard that he can be very kind—that he often shows good and generous feelings. I believe there are people who have reasons to be deeply grateful to him. It is true that he has no religion, but there is, perhaps, nothing very uncommon in that. He goes through the forms of his Church. This is all that is expected from persons in his position.'

'Had you been acquainted with the details of the Czar's life, Madame de Moldau, with its degrading immorality and its brutal coarseness, you would not be deluded into admiration by the brilliant side of his character.'

'I did not speak of what was brilliant, but of what I have heard of his kindness.'

'He was kind to me,' d'Auban said,—'very kind to me once. I had hoped to devote my life to his service. I tried to look on the grand side of his character, on the prodigious results of his genius. I entered into his views, felt proud of his notice.'

'And what happened then? You lost his favour?'

'No; he did not change; I did. Ah! Madame, there are moments in a man's life he cannot speak of without emotion.'

'Far be it from me to intrude on your recollections,' said Madame de Moldau. 'In this new world the past should not be reverted to.'

'Why so, Madame de Moldau? Because we have left behind us country and friends, because we are cut off from old associations, and our lot is cast amidst new interests and new scenes, why should we bury in silence all past reminiscences, and make graves of our memories?'

'That was not my meaning,' she said, 'but only that I did not wish to ask indiscreet questions.'

'You need have no fears of that kind,' d'Auban answered, with a frank smile. 'My life has been full of vicissitudes, but there have been no secrets in it.'

A burning blush overspread Madame de

Moldau's face; she coloured to the very roots of her hair. M. de Chambelle, who was slaughtering mosquitoes, turned round and saw that she looked agitated. He said a few words to her in German. She nodded assent, and then apologised to d'Auban for leaving him. ' I am very tired,' she said ; ' but it is not you who have tired me,' she quickly added ; ' only I have been out of the habit of talking lately. Are we not very silent people, my dear old father ?'

M. de Chambelle, as he opened the door for her, answered this question by a sad and wistful look, and an inclination of the head.

During the ensuing hour d'Auban thought he did not deserve to be ' taxed for silence,' but rather checked for speech. He chattered with the happy talent some people possess of talking immensely. without leaving on the listener's mind any definite idea as to what they have been saying. Twice during that time his daughter sent for him, and on both occasions he instantly obeyed the summons.

As he accompanied his guest on his way home he said to him : ' I wish we could find a French or German servant to wait on

Madame de Moldau. You do not, I suppose, know of such a person?'

'No, indeed, I do not. There are so few respectable European women in these settlements. I wonder if the bargeman Simon's daughter could be induced to accept the situation?'

'What! the black-eyed young lady who acts as stewardess during the voyage? My dear sir, she would indeed be a treasure. Madame de Moldau took quite a fancy to her, I remember. Pray open negotiations with that young individual.'

'As soon as Maitre Simon returns from the Arkansas, where he went with some travellers a few days ago, I will see what can be done.'

During the following week d'Auban sent game and fish and fruit and flowers to St. Agathe, and received in return courteous messages, and at last a little note from Madame de Moldau.

'Sir,—I see you mean to compel me to admire the forests, fields, and streams which furnish the luxuries you send me. I am obliged to admit that nature has lavished her gifts on this favoured region, and that if its aspect is mountainous its productions are full of beauty and variety. Accept my best thanks, and the assurance of my sincere regard.   'C. DE M.'

He sometimes strolled by the river-side and through the neighbouring thickets, in the hope that the lady of St. Agathe would resume her evening walks in the direction of the village, and that he might find an opportunity of introducing her to Father Maret and Thérèse. But she seemed to have lost all taste for walking, and he had not seen her since the day he dined there, neither in the garden or at the window. But one morning M. de Chambelle called and asked him to pay his daughter a visit without letting her know that he had begged him to do so.

'It would give me great pleasure,' he answered; 'but I am sure Madame de Moldau, though she is very kind and civil to me, much prefers my staying away.'

He would have been very sorry not to be contradicted, for he longed to be sitting again in the little drawing-room at St. Agathe, watching the varying expression of the lady's

most expressive countenance, and, as it were,
feeling his way as he approached any new
subject of conversation. A white jessamine
encircled by a fringe of sensitive leaves would
be a fitting emblem, he thought, of the mistress of St. Agathe. He had once amused
himself in by-gone years in overcoming the
shyness of a beautiful Italian greyhound, one
of those delicate creatures who are afraid of
the notice they court, and shrink from a
caress as from a blow. He remembered how
pleased he was the first time Flora conde-
scended to take a bit of biscuit from his hand.
and then laid on his arm her slender snow-
white paw, as a hint she wanted more. He
could not help smiling at the analogy between
those efforts to win the good graces of the
four-footed beauty, and his present endeavours to induce Madame de Moldau to feel
at her ease with him. He was pleased when
M. de Chambelle said, ' If she once gets used
to your society, it will become an enjoyment to her, and perhaps you would be able
to persuade her not to sit all day at the window gazing on the view, and never uttering
a word. Is there nothing we could do to
amuse her?'

The notion of amusement in the kind of life they were leading was a novel one to d'Auban, and he was not prepared to answer the question at once. But after thinking a little he said:

'If she cared for fine scenery we might row her in my boat to the Falls some way up the river—to what the Indians call the Minne Haha or Laughing Water, or perhaps it might interest her to form a collection of birds at St. Agathe. You might have an aviary here without much trouble. But as she does not care for flowers, neither would birds be any pleasure to her I am afraid, nor scenery either.'

'She used to like flowers. Never mind what she says; I see she is pleased when you send her a nosegay. And the fish yesterday was very good. She dined upon it, and thought it the best thing she had tasted since we came here. I wish she would sometimes take a walk. She walked too much when we were at the German village, but now she says it tires her.'

'Would she ride?'

'Ah! she used to delight in it; but how could we get a suitable horse for her?'

'I think one of mine would carry her very well if we could procure a side-saddle. There are beautiful glades in the forest. We might accompany her on foot, or I would lend you my pony.'

M. de Chambelle's face lengthened at this suggestion. 'I am but a poor horseman,' he said. 'Still, if she wished it. But do you think we could catch a squirrel? I saw her watching one yesterday, when we were sitting at the window.'

'Your young negro would be charmed, I dare say, to attempt its capture.'

'Ah, I dare say he would. And will you come and see her to-day?'

'I am obliged to visit a distant part of your plantation; you have doubled my business, you know.'

'Oh dear, how tired you must be!' exclaimed M. de Chambelle in a compassionate tone.

D'Auban laughed.

'Not at all, I assure you. I only meant that I was not much burthened with leisure; but if I am not too late, I will do myself the honour of calling at St. Agathe on my way home.'

CHAPTER IV.

Oh ! deep is a wounded heart, and strong
A voice that cries against mighty wrong ;
And full of death, as a hot wind's blight,
Doth the ire of a crushed affection light.

Mrs. Hemans.

Oh ! there never was yet so pretty a thing
By racing river or bubbling spring—
Nothing that ever so merrily grew
Up from the ground when the skies were blue—
Nothing so fresh, nothing so free,
As thou— my wild, wild cherry-tree.

Barry Cornwall.

The blessing fell upon her soul:
  Her angel by her side
Knew that the hour of grace was come ;
  Her soul was purified.   *Adelaide Proctor.*

D'Auban's business was quickly despatched
that day. He galloped back across the prairie
faster than usual, and dismounting at the foot
of the hill of St. Agathe, he left his horse to
make his way home, and walked to the
pavillon. The heat had been oppressive,
but a refreshing breeze was now beginning

to stir the leaves and to ripple the surface of
the river. The first thing he saw on approaching the house was M. de Chambelle and his
ally Sambo carrying a couch across the lawn.
They placed it in the shade of some wide-
spreading trees, and the former beckoned to
him to join them.

'Oh, what a beautiful nosegay!' he exclaimed. 'Run, Sambo, run, and get a vase
filled with water and a little table from the
parlour. Your bouquet will give an *air de
fête*, dear M. d'Auban, to our *salon d'été*.
Look what a magnificent dome of verdure
and what a soft mossy carpet we have got
here. She is coming in a moment to breathe
a little fresh air. It has been so hot to-day.'

He gave a delighted look at his little
arrangements, and then said he would fetch
his daughter; but when half-way to the
house he turned back to whisper to d'Auban.
'She will not care about the birds, I think;
but I should not be surprised if she was
to allow herself to be rowed in the boat
some day. She said Laughing Water was a
pretty name for a waterfall.' Then he went
off again, and d'Auban sat down on the grass,

musing over the half-provoking, half-amusing manner in which M. de Chambelle presupposed his interest and enlisted his services in his daughter's behalf. 'The poor old man,' he thought, 'seems to take it for granted everyone must share his infatuation.' But when she appeared on the lawn, and he was greeted by her beautiful smile and heard again the sound of her sweet voice, the ungracious feeling vanished. He no longer wondered; on the contrary, it seemed to him quite natural that he and everyone else in the world should be expected to pay her homage. She sat down and said to her father, 'Will you get a chair for M. d'Auban?'

'Not for the world,' d'Auban cried; 'the grass is my favourite seat. But where will *you* sit, M. de Chambelle?' he asked in rather a pointed manner.

She blushed a little and made room for her father by her side; but he said he would do like M. d'Auban and sit on the grass. After a few minutes' conversation about the plantation which they had just purchased, Madame de Moldau asked him to fetch her fan which she had left in the verandah.

'I am afraid, sir,' she then said, addressing d'Auban, 'that you have undertaken for our sakes a heavy amount of labour.'

'Madame,' he answered, 'I am not afraid of labour, and if I can succeed in furthering your interests and relieving you from anxiety, I shall be amply repaid for my exertions. May I hope that you are becoming reconciled to this new world, which must have seemed to you so desolate at first? Are you beginning to take an interest in its natural beauties, and to think you could find happiness in this solitude?'

'What pleases me most in it is its solitude, and I do not think of the future at all. Is not that what moralists say is wisdom, M. d'Auban?'

'Sufficient unto the day is the evil thereof,' he answered, with a smile. 'The Bible teaches us that morality. But man cannot live without hope, earthly or heavenly.'

'I don't think so, or I should have died long ago.' These last words were uttered in so low a voice that he did not hear them, and then, as if to change the subject, she said: 'Nothing could have been so ad-

vantageous to my poor father as this partnership with you.   He has not, I suppose, the
least idea of business?'

'Not much, Madame.   But he furnishes
capital, an important item.'

Madame de Moldau coloured as if about to
say something which cost her an effort. 'Are
you sure, M. d'Auban, that you have not
done yourself an injustice—that your agreement with him is quite a fair one? I know he
would not take advantage of your kindness,
but he might not know——'

'You need have no fears on this point,
Madame.   The agreement is a perfectly reasonable one.   I assure you that we colonists
are very sharp-sighted about our interests.'

'Then I am satisfied;' and she fell into one
of the dreamy reveries which seemed habitual
to her.

He interrupted it by saying, 'May I venture, Madame, to ask you the same question
you put to me just now? What have you
been doing to-day?'

'Only what Italians say it is sweet to do—
nothing.'

'And do you find it sweet?'

'Not in the German settlement, but here 'I rather like it.'

'You must want rest after your dreadful voyage. I wonder you had the courage to undertake it.'

'I am not much afraid of anything;' and then, as if wishing once more to turn the conversation into another channel, she said, 'I interrupted you the other day when you were about to tell me why you left Russia. I should very much like to hear what induced you to do so.'

'I have seldom spoken of the circumstances which compelled me to it. When first I returned to France, my feelings on the subject were too acute, and here you can already perceive that there is scarcely anyone with whom intimate conversation is possible. I had almost forgotten, Madame de Moldau, what it is to converse with a lady of cultivated mind and refined manners, and you can scarcely conceive what a new pleasure it is to one who for five years has lived so much alone, or with uncongenial companions.'

'I can believe it,' she said in a low voice.

'It is not the heart only which has need of

sympathy. The mind also sometimes craves for it.'

Her father returned at that moment with the fan. 'Shall I fan you?' he asked as she held out her hand for it.

'No, thank you. There is more air now. But will you write that letter we were talking about just now? M. d'Auban will call you if I should want anything; but as the barge may go this evening, it ought to be ready.'

'Of course it ought,' answered M. de Chambelle, and again he shuffled away with as much alacrity as before.

Madame de Moldau followed him with her eyes and said. 'What a weight you have taken off his mind, M. d'Auban! He is quite another man since you have undertaken our affairs.'

'How devotedly he loves you,' d'Auban said with much feeling.

'He is indeed devotedly attached to me; no words can do justice to what his kindness has been.' As she uttered these words, Madame de Moldau leant back her head against the cushion and closed her eyes. But tears forced their way through the closed eyelids.

D'Auban gazed silently at those trickling tears, and wondered whence they flowed. Were they bitter as the waters of Marah, or did they give evidence of a grief too sacred to be invaded? He ventured to say in a very low voice, 'You have suffered a great deal,' but she either did not or pretended not to hear him.

'You were going to tell me why you left Russia,' she observed, in a somewhat abrupt tone.

He felt that the best way of winning her confidence would be to be open himself with her as to his own history and feelings.

'My prospects at the court of Russia,' he began, 'were in every way promising; I had reason to believe that the Emperor was favourably disposed towards me. General Lefort was kindness itself. I had lately been appointed to the command of a regiment. I must tell you that some time after my arrival at St. Petersburg, I had made an acquaintance with a young Russian lady whose father had a place at Court. Her name was Anna Vladislava. She was handsome — I thought so, at least—and at the same time was full of genius, wit, and youthful impetuosity.

Hers was a fiery nature which had never known much control. She was fanatically attached to the customs and traditions of her country. We disagreed about everything, religion, politics, books. We never met but we quarrelled. I was one of those foreigners whom, as a class, she held in abhorrence, and yet, strange to say, an attachment sprang up between us. The fearless independence of her character attracted me. It was a refreshing contrast with the servile, cringing spirit of the Czar's Court. She endeavoured to convert me to the orthodox religion, as it is called' (a faint scornful smile curled Madame de Moldau's lip), 'and used to get exasperated at my obduracy. Still in the height of our disputes we behaved to each other as enemies, who were to be one day even more than friends. There was a mutual understanding between us, but no open engagement; of marriage we did not venture to speak. It would have endangered her father's position and prospects, and my own also, to have acknowledged such an intention. I had been given to understand that my imperial master had fixed upon a wife for me, and

to have chosen one myself would have been
a mortal offence ; but we often met, and
though our opinions continued as dissimilar
as ever, there were points of sympathy in
our characters, and our mutual attachment
increased.

' I had sometimes been a little anxious
about Anna's freedom of speech. She allowed
herself openly to inveigh against the Czar's
conduct, and to express her dislike to his
innovations. It was with a kind of natural
eloquence peculiar to her that she was wont
to hold forth about the old Muscovite traditions and the deteriorating influence of
foreign manners and habits on the spirit of a
nation. Poor Anna ! poor bright and careless child ! I remember asking her if she
admired the national custom of husbands
beating their wives, typified by the whip,
which formed part of a bride's trousseau. I
see before me her flashing smile. I hear her
eager defence of that trait of patriarchal
simplicity. "A Russian woman," she said,
" gloried in submission, and looked upon her
husband as her master and her lord." How
little fitted she looked for bondage, and yet

I do believe she would have borne anything
from one she loved. But insult, shame, and
torture. . . .'—d'Auban paused an instant.
Madame de Moldau was listening to him, he
felt it, with intense interest. He went on :
' I used to comfort myself by the thought that
the wild sallies of so young a girl could not
bring her into serious trouble, and I was not
aware of the extent to which her imprudence
was carried. When quite a little child she
had been taken notice of by the Princess
Sophia, the Czar's sister, and had retained a
grateful recollection of her kindness. She
considered this Princess as a martyr to the
cause of Holy Russia, and always spoke in
indignant terms of her long imprisonment.
During a lengthened absence I made from
St. Petersburg she became intimate with
some of this ambitious woman's friends, and
was employed to convey letters to her agents.
The Czar's sister was continually intriguing
against her brother and striving to draw the
nobles into her schemes. My poor Anna
was made a tool of by this party ; a plot
was formed, and discovered by the Emperor.
He was once more seized by the mad fury

which possessed him at the time of the Strelitz revolt, and which caused him to torture his rebellious subjects with his own hands, to insult them in their agonies, and plunge into excesses of barbarity surpassing everything on record, even in the annals of heathen barbarity. . . .'

Madame de Moldau raised herself from her reclining posture, and exclaimed, with burning cheeks and some emotion:

'Oh, M. d'Auban, what violent language you use! State necessity sometimes requires, for the suppression of rebellion, measures at which humanity shudders, but——'

'Ah! I had often said that to myself and to others—often tried to palliate these atrocities by specious reasonings. I had made light of the sufferings of others. Time and distance marvellously blunt the edge of indignation. Sophistry hardens the heart towards the victims, and we at last excuse what once we abhorred. But when cruelty strikes home, when the blow falls on our own heart, when the iron is driven into our own soul, then we know, then we feel, then comes the frightful temptation to curse and to kill. . . . Forgive me, I tire, I agitate you—you look pale.'

'Never mind me. What happened?'

'When I returned to St. Petersburg, this was the news that met me. The girl I loved, and whom I had left gay as a bird and innocent as a child—she who had never known shame or suffering—she who had been led astray by others—was dead: and oh, my God, what a death was hers!'

'Was she put to death?' faintly asked Madame de Moldau.

'No, she was not condemned to death. This would have been mercy to one like her. She was scourged by the executioner, and, had she survived, was to be married to a common soldier, and sent to Siberia. But first reason and then life gave way under the shame and horror of her doom. The proud wild heart broke, and my poor Anna died raving mad. Her father was banished, and the house which had been a home to me I found desolate as a grave.'

'You returned immediately to France?'

'My first impulse—a frantic one—was to take the papers I had brought from the

Crimea to the Czar, and to stab him to the heart. May God forgive me the thought, soon disowned, soon repented of ! It was a short madness, wrestled with and overcome on my knees, but when it had passed away nothing remained to me but to quit the country as quickly and as secretly as possible. I knew I could not endure to see the Emperor ; to feel his hand laid familiarly as it had often been on my shoulder, or to witness his violence and coarse pleasantry, would have been torture. I feigned illness, disposed of my property, and effected my escape.'

'And how soon afterwards did you come here ?'

'About a year.'

There was a pause. D'Auban felt a little disappointed that Madame de Moldau made no comment on his story. The next time she spoke, it was to say—' I wonder if suffering softens or hardens the heart ? '

' I suppose that, like the heat of the sun on different substances, it hardens some and softens others. But the more I live, the more clearly I see how difficult is it to talk of suffering and happiness without saying what sounds like nonsense.'

' I do not understand you.'

' What I mean is this: that there is very little happiness or suffering irrespectively of the temper of mind or the physical constitution of individuals. I have seen so many instances of persons miserable in the possession of what would be generally considered as happiness, and others so happy in the midst of acknowledged evils, such as sickness, want, and neglect, that my ideas have quite changed since I thought prosperity and happiness and adversity and unhappiness were synonymous terms.'

' Could you tell me of some of the instances you mean ?'

' I could relate to you many instances of the happy, amidst apparent—aye, and real suffering too. It is not quite so easy to penetrate into the hearts of the prosperous and place a finger on the secret bruise. But has not your observation, Madame de Moldau, furnished you with such examples ?'

' Perhaps so—are you happy ?'

Few but the young, whose lives have been

spent in perpetual sunshine, know quite how to answer this enquiry. With some the fountain of sorrow has been sealed up, built and bridged over by resignation, acquiescence, or simply by time. Its waters have been hallowed or sweetened, or dried up as may be, but it is like stirring the source afresh to put that question to one who has ever known deep suffering. D'Auban hesitated a moment before he answered it.

'I have been happier here,' he said at last, 'than I had ever been before. But it is quite a different kind of happiness from that which I had once looked forward to.'

'Your sufferings must have been terrible at the time you were speaking of. I felt it, M. d'Auban, but I could not at the moment utter a word of sympathy. It is always so with me.' Her lip quivered, and he exclaimed—

'I know one heart which suffering has not hardened.'

'Oh yes!' she answered, with passionate emotion, 'it has—hardened it into stone, and closed it for ever.'

'Well, my dear sir, have you spoken to her

about riding? Have you succeeded in amusing her?' whispered M. de Chambelle to d'Auban. He had finished his letter and hurried back with it from the house. But the conversation was so eager that his approach had not been noticed.

'Tiring her, I am afraid,' said d'Auban; 'but if you will second my proposal I will venture to plead for Bayard, who would carry you, Madame de Moldau, like a chevalier *sans peur et sans reproche.*'

'I should not be myself *sans peur et sans reproche* if I accepted your kind offer. Not, I am afraid, *sans peur* at mounting him, and certainly not *sans reproche* for depriving you of your horse. But I am grateful, very grateful, for all your kindnesses.' Her eyes were raised to his as she said this, with an expression which thrilled through his heart.

When she had taken leave of him, and was returning to the house, followed by M. de Chambelle, the latter turned back again to say, 'You see she is pleased.'

That that fair creature should be pleased seemed the only thing in the world he cared about. 'Let Belinda but smile, and all the world was to be gay.' D'Auban would have liked to see in her more affectionate warmth of manner towards her father ; but he supposed she might be a little spoilt by his overweening affection.

' Above all things, you will not forget to enquire about the black-eyed dame de compagnie.'

M. de Chambelle said this when, for the second time, he returned to d'Auban, after having escorted his daughter to the house. He followed her like her shadow, and she was apparently so used to this as not to notice it.

' I will not fail to do so ; but Simonette is a wayward being, and may very likely altogether reject the proposal.'

' Gold has, however, a wonderful power over Simon, and if you offer high wages, he may persuade his daughter to accept it. What a beautiful night it is !'

This was said as they approached the river, in which the starry sky was tremblingly reflected. The moon was shedding her silvery light on the foliage and the waving grasses on its banks.

' What a fine thing rest is after a day

of labour!' de Chambelle exclaimed as he stretched and smiled with a weary but happy look.

'If you sleep more soundly, M. de Chambelle, for having committed to me the management of your estate, I do from the increase of work it affords me. But we must really try and make your slaves Christians. Suppose we had a temporary chapel, and two priests, if we could get them, to preach a mission on this side of the river; you would not object to it?'

'Not to anything you wish, my dear friend. And it might, perhaps, amuse Madame de Moldau.'

D'Auban could not repress a smile. It seemed quite a new view of the question.

After M. de Chambelle had left him, he remained out late, attracted by the beauty of the night. Though tired, he did not feel inclined to retire to rest. A musing fit was upon him. He had become conscious that evening that he was in danger of falling in love with Madame de Moldau. He had never yet been the better or the happier for this sort of interest in a woman. After the

tragical end of the only person he had really
cared for, he had made up his mind never to
marry.   But this resolution was not likely to
remain proof against the attractions of so
charming a person.   It was the dread of suffering as he had suffered before ; the fear of
disappointment which had led him to form it,
as well as the apparent hopelessness of meeting in the new world in which his destiny
was cast with any woman capable of inspiring
the sort of attachment without which, with
what his friends called his romantic ideas, he
could not understand happiness in marriage.
It seemed the most improbable thing in the
world that a refined, well-educated, beautiful,
and gentle lady, should take up her residence
in a wild and remote settlement, and yet
such a one had unexpectedly come, almost
without any apparent reason, as a visitant
from another sphere.   With her touching
beauty, her secret sorrows, her strange helplessness, and her impenetrable reserve, she
had, as it were, taken shelter by his side, and
was beginning to haunt his waking hours
and his nightly dreams with visions of a
possible happiness, new and scarcely welcome

to one who had attained peace and content-
ment in the solitary life he had so long led.
In the Christian temple reared in the wilderness, in nature's forest sanctuaries, in the huts
of the poor, by the dying bed of the exile,
he had felt the peace he had sought to impart to others reflected in his own bosom.
He had been contented with his fate. He
had assented to the doom of loneliness, and
foresaw nothing in the future between him
and the grave but a tranquil course of duties
fulfilled and privations acquiesced in. If he
sometimes yearned for closer ties than those
of friendship and charity—if recollections of
domestic life such as he remembered it in the
home of his childhood rose before him in
solitary evenings, when the wind made wild
music amidst the pine branches round
his log-built house, and the rolling sound
of the great river reminded him of the
waves breaking on a far-off coast, he would
forthwith plan some deed of mercy, some
act of kindness, the thought of which generally succeeded in driving away these troublesome reminiscences. He felt almost inclined
to be angry with Madame de Moldau for

awakening in him feelings he had not intended ever to indulge again, visions of a kind
of happiness he had tacitly renounced. Who
has not known some time or other in their
lives those sudden reappearances of long-for-
gotten thoughts—the return of those waves
which we fancied had ebbed and been for ever
swallowed up in the great deep, but which
heave up again, and bring back with them
relics of past joys or dreams of future bliss!

Maître Simon's barge was lying at anchor
near the village. It had just landed a party
of emigrants on their way back from the
Arkansas to New Orleans. He was storing
it with provisions for the rest of the voyage,
and was standing in the midst of cases and
barrels, busily engaged in this labour, when
Colonel d'Auban stepped into the boat, bade
him good morning, and enquired after his
daughter. On his first arrival in America he
had made the voyage up the Mississippi in
one of Simon's boats, and the bargeman's
little girl, then a child of twelve years of age,
was also on board. Simonette inherited from
her mother, an Illinois Indian, the dark complexion and peculiar-looking eyes of that race;

otherwise she was thoroughly French and like her father, whose native land was Gascony. From her infancy she had been the plaything of the passengers on his boat, and they were, indeed, greatly in need of amusement during the wearisome weeks when, half imbedded in the floating vegetation of the wide river, they slowly made their way against its mighty current. As she advanced in years, the child became a sort of attendant on the women on board, and rendered them many little services. She was an extraordinary being. Quicksilver seemed to run in her veins. She never remained two minutes together in the same spot or the same position. She swam like a fish and ran like a lapwing. Her favourite amusements were to leap in and out of the boat, to catch hold of the swinging branches of the wild vine, and run up the trunks of trees with the agility of a squirrel, or to sit laughing with her playfellows, the monkeys, gathering bunches of grapes and handfuls of wild cherries for the passengers. She had a wonderful handiness, and a peculiar talent for contrivances. There were very few things Simonette could not do if she once set about them. She twisted ropes of the long grass which grows on the floating islands of the Mississippi, and could build a hut with old boards and pieces of coarse canvass, or prepare a dinner with hardly any materials at all—as far as anyone could see. She mended dresses or made them, kept her father's accounts, or, what was more extraordinary still, proved a clever and patient nurse to the passengers who fell ill with the dreadful fever of the country. Wild as an elf, and merry as a sprite at other times, she would then sit quietly by the side of the sufferers, bathing their foreheads or chafing their hands as the hot or cold fit was upon them, and rendering them every kind of service.

During the time that d'Auban was on board her father's boat, it was the little stewardess herself who fell ill. One day her laugh was no longer heard—the plaything, the bird, the elf, ceased to dart here and there as she was wont to do in the exuberance of her youthful spirits. Nothing had ever before subdued her. She did not know what it was to fear anything, except perhaps a blow from her father, and, to do him justice, his blows were not hard ones. A bit of European finery or a handful of sweetmeats were enough to send her into an ecstasy. Sometimes she was in a passion, but it did not last beyond a minute or two, and she was laughing again before there had been time to notice that she was out of temper. But now sickness laid its heavy hand on the poor child, her aching head drooped heavily on her breast. She did not care for anything, and when spoken to scarcely answered. Simon sat by his little daughter, driving away the insects from her face, and trying in his rough way to cheer her. D'Auban also came and sat by her side, and whispered to him, ' Has she been baptized ? '

' No, I have never had time to take her to a priest.'

D'Auban sighed, and Simon looked at him anxiously. Faith was not quite extinct in him, and grief, as it often does, had revived the dying spark.

' May I briefly instruct, and then baptize her ? ' d'Auban added.

' You ! but you are not a priest.'

'No, but a layman may baptize a person in danger of death.'

The little girl overheard the words, and cried out, 'I will not die ; don't let me die.'

'No, my bird, my little one, you shall not die,' Simon answered, weeping and wringing his hands.

'Not unless the good God chooses to take you to His beautiful home in heaven,' said d'Auban, kneeling by the side of the child. Then he talked to her in a low and soothing voice, and taught her the few great truths she could understand. Then, showing her a crucifix, he made her repeat a simple act of contrition, and baptized her in the name of the Father, the Son, and the Holy Ghost. As the water flowed on her brow she raised her eyes no longer with a wild elfish smile, but a calm contented look. He made her a Christian that day, and on their arrival at the mission of St. Francis he took her to Father Maret, who, whilst her father's bark was repairing, placed her under Thérèse's care. She was christened in the church, and made her first communion before his next voyage. Thérèse took great pains with her charge, but she did not understand her character. The Indian's grave and earnest soul did not harmonise with the volatile, impulsive, and wayward nature of the Frenchman's child. Simonette heard Mass on Sunday, and said short prayers night and morning, but her piety was of the active order. She studied her catechism up in some tree, seated on a branch, or else swinging in one of the nets in which Indian women rock their children. She could hardly sit still during a sermon, and from sheer restlessness envied the birds as they flew past the windows. But if Father Maret had a message to send across the prairie, or if food and medicine was to be carried to the sick, she was his ready messenger—his carrier-pigeon, as he called her. Through tangled thickets and marshy lands she made her way, fording with her naked feet the tributary streams of the great river, or swimming across them if necessary; jumping over fallen trunks, and singing as she went, the bird-like creature made friends and played with every animal she met, and fed on berries and wild honey.

As she grew older, the life she led, her

voyages to and from New Orleans, and above all, the acquaintances she made in that town, were very undesirable for a young girl. She learnt much of the evil of the world, was often thrown into bad company, listened to conversation and read books well adapted to taint the mind and corrupt the heart. But as yet she had passed through these scenes and been exposed to those trials without much apparent bad result. When she returned to St. François du Sault, her manner was for a while bold and somewhat wild; she said foolish and reckless things. But an interview with Father Maret, a few days spent amongst good people, or a word of friendly advice from her godfather, would set her right again, and cause her to resume her good habits, to soften her voice, and sober her exuberant spirits. She had found a safeguard against contaminating influences in a feeling the nature of which she could scarcely have defined, composed as it was of gratitude, admiration, and a love which had in it no admixture of hope or expectation of return. Sometimes these extraneous helps are permitted to do their work and to assist human weakness to keep its footing amidst life's shoals and quicksands—themselves at best but sands! But if a grain of sand has ever stood between us and sin it is not to be despised: nor will He despise it who caused the gourd to grow over the prophet's head, and to wither away when its mission was fulfilled.

'Where is Simonette?' enquired d'Auban, after the first words of civility had passed between him and the bargeman.

'She was here a minute ago,' answered Simon with a grin, ' but that is rather a reason she should not be here now. The girl is never in the same place for two minutes together.'

'What! have not advancing years at all tamed her?' said d'Auban, laughing. ' Is she quite the same light-hearted creature who enlivened for me the horrors of my first acquaintance with your barges, Maître Simon? Well, I am glad of it. In the midst of mournful-looking Indians and careworn settlers, it is pleasant to have a laughing fairy like your daughter to remind us that there still exists such a thing as mirth. But I wish she was

here.   I have something to propose to her.
However, I may as well, perhaps, broach the
subject to you.'

'Is it something profitable?' asked Maître
Simon, thrusting his hands in his pockets.

'It is a situation with a lady.   You will
admit that such an offer is not often to be met
with in this country.'

'What sort of situation?'

'Partly as attendant, partly as companion.'

'And is the lady a real one?'

'I have no doubt she is.'

'And a person of good character?   You
see, Colonel, I am an old sinner myself, but
I should not like my little girl to live with
some of the ladies whom we know come out
to the colony.'

D'Auban felt he had no proof to give of
Madame de Moldau's respectability beyond
his own entire belief in it.

He answered in a somewhat sneering
manner. 'I will engage to say that, as far
as morality goes, she is greatly superior to
the persons your daughter associates with on
board your boats.'

'Ah! but there I watch over her.'

Whatever d'Auban might think of the amount of Simon's parental vigilance, he felt that his own manner of speaking had been wrong.

'All I can tell you is,' he said in a different tone, 'that from what I have myself seen of Madame de Moldau, I am persuaded that she is a person of unexceptionable character. Her father has more fortune than the generality of settlers, and has bought M. de Harlay's pavillon. I did not know them before they came here; but my impressions are so favourable that I do not hesitate to advise you to accept the offer I speak of, if Simonette herself is inclined to do so.'

'Here comes the monkey.' cried Simon, pointing to the thicket from whence his daughter was emerging. 'May I speak to her first about it?' d'Auban asked.

'Certainly; only when you come to talk of wages you better take me into council.'

D'Auban went to meet the girl. In her half-French, half-Indian costume, with her black hair twisted in a picturesque manner round her head, and her eyes darting quick glances. more like those of a restless bird than of a woman, Simonette, as Maitre Simon's daughter had always been called, was rather pretty. There was life, animation, and a kind of brilliancy about her, though there was no real beauty in her features, and no repose in her countenance; she seemed always on the point of starting off, and had a way of looking out of the corner of her eye as if she caught at what was said to her rather than listened to it.

'How do you do, Simonette? It is a long time since I have seen you.'

'Sir, I thought you had forgotten me.'

'No, indeed, I have not; and the proof is in my coming here to-day to offer you a situation.'

'Sir, I don't want a situation.'

'Hear what it is, Simonette, before you decide. Madame de Moldau, the lady at St. Agathe, would like to engage you as an attendant; but, in fact, what she really wants is a companion.'

'Sir, she had better not take me.'

'Why so, Simonette?'

'Because, sir, I should not suit her.'

'But I think you would, Simonette, and I really wish you would think about it.'

'Well, wait a moment, and I will.' She darted off, and in a moment was out of sight.

Maitre Simon came up to d'Auban and asked what had become of her.

'She says she must take time to consider, and has rushed into the thickets.'

'I always maintain she is more like a monkey than a woman,' Simon exclaimed, in a tone of vexation. 'I dare say she is in the hollow of a tree or at the top of a branch. I wish she was married and off my hands. What wages would the lady give?'

'Well, forty francs a month, I suppose.'

'Fifty would be more to the purpose. You see, sir, if it is not often that ladies are to be found in these parts, it is just as seldom that ladies' maids are to be met with.'

'Well, I admit there is something in that. Let us then say fifty.'

'Ah! I know you are a reasonable man, Colonel d'Auban. I wish the girl would come back.'

In a few minutes she did return, holding a small ape in her arms, and playing a thousand tricks with it.

'Well, Simonette, your father is satisfied

about the wages.　It remains for you to say
if you will accept the situation.'

'No, sir, I will not.' answered Simonette,
looking hard into the monkey's face.

'But it is a very good offer,' urged her
father.　'Fifty francs a month.　What are
you thinking of, child?'

'It would also be an act of charity towards the lady,' d'Auban put in.　'She is ill
and sorrowful.'

'And I am sure it would be a charity
to ourselves,' Simon said, in a whining
voice.　'Passengers are not so frequent as
they used to be, and it is like turning our
backs on Providence to refuse an honest employment.'

'It is the lady we brought some months ago,
father, from New Orleans,' said Simonette.
'A pale, tall woman, with blue eyes.'

'Of course, I remember her quite well. The
old gentleman paid my bill without saying a
word, which very few of my passengers have
the right feeling to do.　I am sure they must
be excellent people.'

There was a slight sneer on his daughter's
lip.

'What does this lady expect of me, sir?' she said, turning to d'Auban.

'To help her to govern her household, and render all the little services you can. She is much inclined to like you, and I think you would be very happy at St. Agathe.'

Simonette laughed a short bitter laugh, and, hugging the monkey, whispered in its ear, 'Oh, my good little ape! Are you not glad to see how foolish men can be? Then, suddenly becoming grave, she looked steadily at d'Auban and said, 'Then, sir, you really wish me to accept the offer?'

'I really do. I think it will be a mutual advantage to this lady and to you.'

'Then, God forgive me, I will.'

'God forgive you!' exclaimed d'Auban, puzzled, and beginning to feel irritated with the girl's manner. 'What can you mean?'

'She is in one of her moods; it is the Indian blood in her,' cried Maître Simon. 'But you know, Colonel, she soon gets out of these queer tempers; she is a good girl on the whole. May we consider the affair as settled?'

'1 suppose so,' said d'Auban, speaking rather coldly. 'If you will come to-morrow at nine o'clock to St. Agathe, Simonette, Madame de Moldau will see you.'

'Very well, sir. Have you any other commands for me?'

'No. only to catch and tame for me just such another ape as that.'

'They are not easily tamed. They require a great deal of affection.'

'Oh! that I cannot promise to give to a monkey.'

'The love of a little animal is not to be always despised,' muttered Simonette, ' nor its hatred;' and then she went about the barge pulling things about and exciting the ape to grin and to chatter. When d'Auban and her father had gone away, she sat down on one of the benches and began to cry. 'Oh, bad spirit!' she exclaimed—'fierce spirit of my mother's race, go out of my heart. Let the other spirit return—the dancing, laughing, singing spirit. Oh, that the Christian spirit that took charge of me when I was baptized would drive them both away—I am so tired of their fighting!'

Just then Thérèse came near the boat and said, 'Simonette, all the girls of the mission assemble to-day in the church to renew their baptismal vows, and the chief of prayer will speak to them. The altar is lighted up, and the children are bringing flowers. Will you come?'

Simonette was soon with her companions in the forest chapel, and after the service was over she played with them on the greensward under the tulip trees. The maiden of seventeen summers was as wild with spirits, as turbulent in her glee, as the youngest of the party. She stopped once in the midst of a dance to whisper to Thérèse—'The Indian spirit is gone out of my heart for the present, but as to the French one, if I drive it out at the door it comes back by the window. What is to be done?'

CHAPTER V.

Strive; yet I do not promise
  The prize you dream of to-day
Will not fade when you think to grasp it,
  And melt in your hand away.
Pray, though the gift you ask for
  May never comfort your fears,
May never repay your pleading,
  Yet pray, and with hopeful tears;
And far through the misty future,
  With a crown of starry light,
An hour of joy you know not
  Is winging her silent flight. *Adelaide Proctor.*

Rumour is a pipe blown by surmises, jealousies, conjectures.
  Shakespeare.

On the following morning Colonel d'Auban met Simonette in the avenue of the pavillon. M. de Chambelle was coming out of the house with a very disconsolate countenance. He brightened up a little when he saw d'Auban.

'I do not know what is to become of us,' he said. 'Madame de Moldau is quite ill, and the Indian servant does not know how to do anything. Mon Dieu! what a country this is! Why would she come here?'

'I have brought Maitre Simon's daughter, M. de Chambelle. She wishes to offer her services to Madame de Moldau.'

'Ah! Mademoiselle Simonette, you are a messenger from heaven!'

The celestial visitant was looking at poor M. de Chambelle with an expression which had in it a little too much *malice* to be quite angelic. 'Let Mademoiselle,' he continued, 'name her own terms.' It was fortunate that Simon was not there to hear this, and d'Auban mentioned the sum agreed upon between them. M. de Chambelle gladly assented, and said he would go and inform his daughter of Mademoiselle's arrival. 'I beg you will be seated,' he said, bowing to the young quadroon with as much ceremony as if she had been a princess in disguise.

With equal formality he announced to his daughter that he had found her an attendant in the little stewardess on board the Frenchman's barge.

'Do you mean his daughter?' she asked—

'the girl with eyes as black as the berries she gathered for us?'

'Yes, Madame, the young person who sometimes used to make you laugh.'

'You know, my dear father, we had resolved not to have European servants. I feel as if it would be running a risk.'

'But this girl is a quadroon. She has never been in Europe. She is really half a savage.'

'On the contrary, my good father, she is a very civilised little being—far too much so for us. Indeed, I had rather not take her into the house.'

'But I cannot bear any longer, and that is the real truth, to see you without any of the comforts you ought to have . . . Oh yes, I know the walls are thin. I will not speak too loud. But did I not find you yesterday kneeling on the floor, trying to make the fire burn, and that horrible squaw standing stupidly by?'

'It is not the poor creature's fault; she is willing to learn.'

'And in the meantime you, you, my own——'

The old man burst into tears, and leant

against the foot of the bed overpowered with grief. 'If you knew what I suffer when I see you thus!'

'Poor old father! do not grieve. There have been times when I have suffered much more than I do now. And let this thought be a comfort to you. What should I have done but for your care? I sometimes, however, ask myself if it was worth while to go through so much in order to lead such a life as this. If it would not have been better——' She hid her face in her hands and shuddered. 'No, no, I am not ungrateful. But do not take it unkindly, dear good father, if I talk to you so little. I often feel like a wounded animal who cares for nothing but to lie down exhausted. I remember—ah! I had resolved never to use that word again—but I do remember seeing a stricken deer lying on the grass, in a green valley near the tower where the hounds used so often to meet. It was panting and bleeding. I could not help weeping, even as you are now weeping. Dear old father! try not to give way to grief. It only makes me sad. Settle as you think best about this French or Indian girl. Does Colonel d'Auban recommend us to take her?'

'Most strongly. He is sure you will find her useful. He feels as I do ; he cannot bear to see you without proper attendance.'

'You have not told him!'

'Heaven forbid! but anybody would be sorry to see you so ill and with no one to nurse you.'

'Well, let her come. I have not energy enough to resist yours and his kind wishes. The future must take its chance. But before you go, lock up that book, if you please.'

This was the volume of German Psalms which had been snatched out of d'Auban's hand on the day of his first visit.

There was an undefinable expression in Simonette's face when she came into Madame de Moldau's room—an uneasy suspicious look. She answered briefly the questions put to her, and seemed relieved when her active exertions were called into play. She had not been many hours in the house before it assumed a new aspect. Some people have a natural talent for making others comfortable, and relieving the many little sources of disquietude which affect invalids.

Madame de Moldau's couch was soon furnished with cushions made of the dried willow grass, which the Indians collect for a similar purpose. The want of blinds or shutters was supplied by boughs, ingeniously interwoven and fixed against the windows. The sunbeams could not pierce through the soft green of these verdant curtains. The kitchen was put on a new footing, and towards evening a French *consommé* was brought to Madame de Moldau, such as she had not tasted since her arrival in America.

' I could not have believed a basin of broth could ever have been so acceptable,' she said with a kind smile when her new attendant came to fetch the cup away.

Simonette made no answer. Her manner to her mistress was by no means agreeable ; she laboured indefatigably for her, but the gaiety which had been her principal attraction only showed itself now by fits and starts. She soon became the ruling power at St. Agathe; took all trouble off M. de Chambelle's hands, and managed him as a child. The Indian servant.

the negro boy, and even the slaves on the plantation, owned her sway. After she had been at the pavillon about three weeks, D'Auban met her and said, 'Your employers are delighted with you, Simonette.'

'They would do better to send me away, sir,' she testily replied.

'Why so?' he asked, feeling hurt and disappointed.

'Sir, I do not like people who have secrets.'

'What do you mean?'

Before she could answer M. de Chambelle joined them, and she went away. The recklessness of her childhood, and the exuberance of her animal spirits, had now taken the form of incessant activity. She never seemed happy except when hard at work.

D'Auban's visits to St. Agathe were becoming more and more frequent. There were few evenings he did not end his rounds by spending a few moments under the verandah or in the parlour of the pavillon. Most of his books, and all his flowers gradually made their way there. Antoine, though little given to reading himself, bitterly complained that there was

scarcely a volume left on his master's shelves.
He began to feel at home in that little room,
to which Simonette had contrived to impart
an Old World look of comfort. Her glimpses
of the colonists' houses at New Orleans had
given her an insight into European habits.
His chair was placed for him between Madame
de Moldau and her father, and, though she
was habitually silent, the hours glided by with
wonderful rapidity during the now lengthen-
ing evenings, as he recounted the little incidents of the day, or described the scenery he
had rode through, or dwelt on the new plans
he was forming. She always listened with
interest to everything he said, but did not
seem to care much about the people amongst
whom their lot was cast. The mention of
any kind of suffering always made her shudder,
but that negroes, Indians, or poor people of
any sort were of the same nature as herself,
she did not seem exactly to realise. Practi-
cally, she did not care much more about them
than for the birds and beasts, living and dying
around her in the sunshine and the shade.
But d'Auban, by telling her facts which came
home to her woman's heart, gradually awoke

in her a new sense of sympathy. It was dangerous ground, however, to venture on, for if the woes of others did not always appear to touch her deeply, yet sometimes the mention of them provoked a burst of feeling which shook her delicate frame almost to pieces. M. de Chambelle on these occasions was wont to look at him reproachfully, and at her with a distressed expression till she had recovered her composure. D'Auban also got into the habit of watching every turn of her countenance, every tone of her voice. She attracted and she puzzled him. Not only did her father, and she herself, continue to preserve a nearly total silence as to their past history, but there were peculiarities in her character he did not understand. It was impossible in many ways to be more amiable, to show a sweeter disposition, or bear with more courage the privations and discomforts she was often subjected to. But he could not help observing that, notwithstanding all her sweetness and amiability, she took it as a matter of course that her wishes should be considered paramount to any other considera-tion. She acknowledged Simonette's services with kindness, but made ample, and not always very considerate, use of them. He was often sent for himself at inconvenient times, and for somewhat trifling reasons, and she did not seem to understand that the requirements of business were imperious, and could not be postponed to suit her convenience. But he was so glad to see her shake off the listless despondency which had weighed upon her during the first period of her residence at St. Agathe, so delighted to hear her express any wish and take pleasure in anything; the least word of thanks from her had such a charm for him, and ministering to her happiness was becoming so absorbing an interest, that, even whilst wondering at M. de Chambelle's paternal infatuation, he was fast treading in his footsteps, and in danger of being himself subjected to the same gentle tyranny. Their conversations grew longer and more intimate. He felt he was gaining influence over her. Often when he was expressing his opinions on various subjects, she would say:

' I had never thought of that before ;' or, ' it had never struck me in that light.' And he would notice the result of some observation he had made in slight changes in her conduct.

There was one subject, however, she always carefully avoided, and that was religion. He was in total ignorance as to her feelings and opinions on that point. Except the volume of German Psalms which had been taken out of his hand, he had seen nothing at St. Agathe which gave him any idea as to the form of religion she professed, or whether she held any religious belief at all. At last he resolved to break silence on this subject by putting a direct question to her.

This happened one evening when he had been speaking of the slaves, and of the measures he was taking for their instruction in Christianity. He abruptly asked, 'What is your religion, Madame de Moldau?'

The silence which ensued was painful to both. His heart was beating very fast, and an expression of annoyance almost amounting to displeasure was visible in her face. At last, as he seemed to persist in expecting an answer, she said, 'I think I should be justified in refusing to answer that question.

There are subjects on which, in such a country as this at least, thought may be free. I would rather not be questioned as to my religious belief.'

'Forgive me, Madame de Moldau, but is this a friendly answer? Do you think it is curiosity leads me to ask? Do you think, as day after day we have sat talking of everything except religion, that I have not longed to know what you thought—what you believed? . . . No, I will not let you be silent. I will not leave you till you have answered my question.'

There was in d'Auban's character the strength of will which gives some persons a natural ascendancy over others. Other qualities may contribute to it, but determination is the natural element of all such power. It has also been said that in any friendship or intimacy between two persons, there comes a moment which establishes the ascendancy of one of the parties over the other; and if this be true, that moment was arrived for those we are now speaking of. Madame de Moldau had resolved not to open her lips on the subject which he was equally determined she should speak upon. She wept and made signs that he should leave her; but he who had been hitherto subservient to her slightest wish, who had treated her with an almost exaggerated deference, now stood firm to his point. He sat resolutely on with his lips compressed, his dark grey eyes fixed upon her, and his whole soul bent on obtaining the answer which he hoped would break down the wall of silent misery rising between her soul and the consolations she so much needed.

'Madame de Moldau, what religion do you *profess?*' he again asked, laying a stress on the last word.

'I profess none,' she answered in a voice stifled with sobs.

'Well, then, thank God that you have said so—that you have had the courage to avow the truth. If you would only open your heart——'

'Open my heart!' she repeated, with a melancholy emphasis. 'You do not know what you are saying; I am not like other people.'

'But will you not tell me, Madame, in what religion you were educated?'

A bitter expression passed over her face as she answered—

'In no particular religion.'

'Is this possible?'

'I was always told it did not signify what people believed, and, God knows, I think so now.'

'Madame, is that your creed?'

'I detest all creeds.'

'And have you never practised any religion?'

'I have gone through certain forms.'

'Those of the Catholic religion?'

Madame de Moldau was silent.

'For heaven's sake, Madame, answer that one question.'

'No, I have never been a Catholic.'

'Oh, I am so glad!'

'Why so?'

'You will not understand it now, Madame, but some day you will. And now, before I go, do tell me that I have not offended you.'

'I ought, perhaps, to be offended, but in truth I cannot say that I am. Perhaps it is because I cannot afford to quarrel with the only friend I have in the world.' She held out her hand, and for the first time he pressed it to his lips.

'And I suppose I am to read these books?' she said, with a faint smile, pointing to the last volumes he had sent. 'I doubt not they are carefully chosen.'

'There was not much to choose from in my library, and no art in the selection. I have sent you the friends which have strengthened me in temptation, consoled me in sorrow, and guided me through life.'

As he was leaving Madame de Moldau's room, D'Auban perceived through the green leaves two eyes fixed upon them. He wondered who it was was watching them, and darted out to see. Simonette was sitting at work in the verandah, humming the old French song:

Au clair de la lune,
Mon ami Pierrot,
Prête-moi ta plume,
Pour écrire un mot.

'Who was looking into that room?' he said, going up to her in an angry manner.

She shrugged her shoulders without answering. He felt convinced it must have been her eyes he had seen through the green boughs, but thought it better not to say so.

'Do you like your situation, Simonette?' he asked.

'No, sir, I do not.'

'Are you not well treated?'

'I have nothing to complain of.'

'What makes you dislike it, then?'

'Nothing that anybody can help.'

'Come, Simonette, I am an old friend of yours. You ought to speak to me with more confidence.'

'A friend to me! yes, you have indeed been the best of friends to a friendless girl; but, sir, it was not a friendly act to bring me here.'

'I wish you would speak plainly.'

'That is just what I cannot do.'

'You are not used to service, and find it irksome, I suppose?'

'No, I have always served some one or other since I can recollect.'

'Your mistress seems particularly kind to you, and I know both she and her father are greatly pleased with your services.'

'And it gives you pleasure that I should stay here?'

This was said in a gentler tone of voice.

'Well, I should be glad that you remained, and I cannot see any reason against it.'

'Then, sir, I will try to do so,' she answered, in a humble, submissive manner. 'Good-bye, M. d'Auban.'

When he was gone, the young girl sank down again on the seat, and for a moment covered her face with her hands. When she took up her work again, and as her eyes wandered over the lawn, they caught sight of something yellow and glittering lying on the grass, at a short distance from the house. She went to pick it up, and found a magnificent gold locket, which contained a miniature set in diamonds. She held it open on the palm of her hand, and gazed alternately at the picture and on the words inscribed at the back. An expression of surprise, a sort of suppressed exclamation, rose from her compressed lips; then putting it in her pocket, she walked back to the house—not in her usual darting bird-like fashion, but slowly, like a person whose mind is wholly absorbed. Madame de Moldau had been asking for her, and when she came in complained a little of her absence; but, observing that she looked ill, kindly enquired if she was ailing.

'You work too hard, perhaps. I really do not think you ever take a moment's rest. I reproach myself for not having noticed it before.'

'Indeed, you need not do so, lady, for it is not for your sake that I came here, and if I do spend my strength in working for you, neither is it for your sake that I do so.'

Madame de Moldau coloured a little, for there was something offensive in the tone with which this was said.

'Do you mean,' she asked with a slight amount of irony, 'that it is all for the love of God, as pious people say?'

'No, Madame; Thérèse works in that way, and I wish with all my heart I did so too. She has no master but the good God.'

'And for whom do you work, then? Who do you call your master? Is it the priest, or your own father?'

'I am not speaking of them, Madame.'

'Then of whom are you speaking?'

'May not I have my secrets, Madame, as you have yours?'

Madame de Moldau coloured deeply, and put her hand to her heart as if to still its throbbings.

'Call M. de Chambelle,' she faintly said.

'He is gone out, Madame, with M. d'Auban. I saw them crossing the stream a moment ago.'

Madame de Moldau sighed deeply, and joined her hands together in an attitude of forced endurance. Simonette was looking at her with a searching glance. One of her hands was in her pocket tightly grasping the locket she had found. At last she said:

'Lady, have you lost anything?'

Madame de Moldau hurriedly felt for the black ribbon round her neck, and not finding it there, turned pale.

'What have you found?' she asked.

'A very beautiful trinket,' Simonette answered, and pulled the locket out of her pocket. 'Of course it belongs to you,

Madame? Those are larger diamonds than any I have yet seen, but I learnt at New Orleans the value of those kind of things.'

Madame de Moldau held out her hand for the locket. 'Thank you,' she quickly said. 'It is my property.' Then she took off a small ring and offered it to her attendant. 'This is not a reward for your honesty, for I am sure you do not wish for one, but rather a token of the pleasure it gives me to recover this locket.'

Simonette hesitated. On the one hand the thought crossed her mind, that the offer of the ring was a bribe. She thought she had grounds for thinking this possible. The conflict which had been going on in her mind since her coming to St. Agathe seemed to have reached a crisis. 'I am much obliged to you, Madame,' she said at last, 'but I would rather not accept this ring.'

A long silence ensued. Both took up some needlework. The hands of the mistress trembled, whilst her attendant's fingers moved with nervous rapidity. After a long silence the former said, 'You have been a kind and a useful attendant, Simonette, and I do not

know what I should have done without you
during my illness; but I am now quite
recovered. You do not seem to be happy
here, and I ought to learn to wait on myself.
Is it not better that we should part?'

Again good and bad thoughts of that gentle
lady passed like lightning through the girl's
mind. 'She wishes to get rid of me. She
knows I suspect her. Perhaps I am an
obstacle to some of her wicked plans.' The
indignant inward voice was answered by
another. 'It is cruel to suspect her. Cruel
to leave her. She will be ill again if I go. At
the bottom of my heart I believe I love her.'

She raised her eyes, which she had hitherto
kept fixed on her work. Madame de Moldau
was weeping; she looked the very picture of
youthful and touching sorrow—so innocent,
so gentle, so helpless. Their eyes met, and
Simonette's were also full of tears. 'Would
you be sorry to leave me, Simonette?'

'M. d'Auban will be very angry with me
if I do.'

'Not if I chose to part with you?'

This was said with gentleness but firmness.

Simonette felt her conduct was ungenerous, and she exclaimed, 'I have been wrong; do let me stay, Madame. I cannot bear that M. d'Auban should think me ungrateful.'

'What has he done to inspire you with so much gratitude?'

'What has he *not* done for me?' Simonette replied, with deep emotion. 'I was an outcast and he reclaimed me—a savage and he instructed me—I was dying, and he baptized me!'

'Indeed! When?—where?'

'Five years ago in my father's boat. I had the fever. I shall never forget the words he said to me then, or what I felt when he poured the water on my head.'

'And he has been kind to you ever since?'

'Oh yes, very kind; he is always kind.'

'He has, indeed, been so to us.'

'May I stay?'

'I don't know, Simonette; M. de Chambelle will decide.'

'Then I am sure I shall stay.'

This was said in a tone which, in the midst

of her emotion, which had not yet subsided, made Madame de Moldau laugh. That laugh settled the question. But, although Simonette's heart had been touched, her mind was not satisfied. The sight of the locket and of the picture it contained stood between her and her peace. She took advice of Father Maret. He, probably, was of opinion that she should stay at St. Agathe, for she said nothing more about leaving; but though she grew every day fonder of her mistress, it was clear that some secret anxiety was preying on her mind.

After this day nothing occurred for some time to disturb the even course of the settlers' lives. D'Auban now spent all his spare time at St. Agathe, and Madame de Moldau gradually began to take an interest in his pursuits and occupations. The united concessions were flourishing under his management, and the condition of the labourers rapidly improving. At last she was induced to visit some of the huts on the plantation, and as soon as the effort was made, she found pleasure in doing good to her poor neighbours and in studying how to help them—first, by furnishing them with little comforts such as they could appreciate, and then by nursing them in sickness. But when it came to this she felt her own helplessness in cases where persons were troubled in mind, or leading bad lives, or plunged in ignorance. Her own ideas were too vague, her own belief too uncertain, to enable her to give advice or consolation to others. One day she found Thérèse in a cabin where a Frenchman was lying at the point of death. She had spoken to her two or three times before, and d'Auban had been anxious to make them better acquainted, but they were both very reserved, and no advance had been made towards intimacy. Wishing not to disturb her she remained near the door, and did not make her presence known. Thérèse was speaking earnestly to the sick man and preparing him for the last sacrament, which Father Maret was soon to bring him. What she said, simple as it was, indeed, because of its simplicity, made a great impression on Madame de Moldau. It gave her different ideas about religion than she had hitherto had. She remained in that poor hut watching, for the first time in her life, the approach of death, and with all sorts of new thoughts crowding into her mind. She placed on the floor the provisions she had brought with her, and slipped away unperceived; but the next day Thérèse was surprised by a visit from the lady of St. Agathe, and still more so by her saying, ' Thérèse, you must instruct me in your religion.'

A thrill of joy ran through the Indian's heart, but she answered, ' Not so, daughter of the white man. Let me take you to the black robe.'

' Not yet, Thérèse, not yet. You must teach me yourself, and then perhaps I will go to the black robe.'

' But the eagle of your tribe—he can tell you more than a poor Indian about the Great Spirit and the Christian's prayer.'

' Are you speaking of Colonel d'Auban, Thérèse ? '

' Yes, of the great and good chief of the white men. They call him amongst us the great hunter and the strong arm, but it is his goodness makes him a son of the Great Spirit, and the hope of all who suffer.'

' It is his goodness which began to make

me think of learning your religion, Thérèse; but it is you who must teach me.'

She would take no denial. Day after day the European lady sat by the side of the daughter of an Algonquin chief in her poor hut, and learnt from her lips the lessons taught from the time of the Apostles by simple and learned men, by poor monks and great divines, in universities and village schools, in the cathedrals of Old Europe and the forest chapels of the New World. She drank in the spirit of child-like piety which breathed in all that Thérèse did and said, and never felt so peaceful as in her cottage. There no questions were raised which could agitate her, no allusions were made to the past, no anxious looks were bent upon her. D'Auban's affection, as well as Simonette's curiosity, were ever on the watch. They were all more or less watching one another. She was not ungrateful for his solicitude, but it sometimes seemed to weary her. There was a struggle going on between them, and also, perhaps, in her own heart. He was always trying to break through the barrier which, with all her feeble womanly strength, she was resolutely keeping closed.

Thérèse, on the contrary, cared nothing for her past history, had no wish to know who she was and whence she came. Her only object was to make her love the Christian prayer and serve the Great Spirit with as much zeal as herself. This simple and ardent faith, joined to the daily example of her holy life, had more effect on her disciple than able arguments or deep reasonings. The books she had lately read at d'Auban's request had doubtless removed some prejudices from her mind and prepared the way for the reception of dogmatic truth ; but it was not Bossuet's writings, nor St. François de Sale's, the most persuasive of Christian writers, that finally overcame her scepticism and converted her to Catholicism. When she heard the young Indian girl speaking of the honour and joy of dying for one's faith, and envying the terrible sufferings which some of her countrymen had not long ago endured for the sake of their religion, it served to convince her far more than abstract reasonings that a creed is not a mere symbol or religion a set of particular ceremonies. She saw in Thérèse how a young person can sacrifice for the love of God everything that is commonly called happiness and pleasure ; and that, amidst the untutored savages of the New World, as well as formerly amongst the proud and luxurious Roman nobles, Christians lay down their lives gladly for the sake of their faith ; and this more than anything else showed her the difference between an opinion and a creed, a sentiment and a religion. Though she did not converse with freedom on these subjects with d'Auban, she liked to hear from Thérèse of his love of the poor, of his tenderness towards the sick and aged. She knew that priests and sisters of charity cared for the poor, but that a man in the prime of life, full of ability and talent, should cherish the outcasts of the human race—savages and slaves—was first a wonder and then a new light to her. Thérèse's imagination, fraught with imagery and tinged with enthusiasm, drew pictures of his goodness which had in them truth as well as beauty. She described how the white man, who could hunt and swim and slay the leopard and the wolf, and conquer in battle the greatest warriors of the

four nations, loved little children and carried
them in his arms. She said he was like the
west wind walking lightly over the prairies,
whispering to the lilies.

Madame de Moldau listened, and her blue
eyes, which seemed often fixed in mournful
contemplation on invisible scenes of sorrow,
would suddenly light up as if a brighter
vision rose before them. She was at last
persuaded one evening to attend a service
in the church of the Mission. It was one of
those at which the negroes from the neighbouring plantations usually flocked. Hidden
in a recess, she heard the black robe preach
to the poor slaves. He spoke of the weary
and heavy laden, of a bondage sadder than
theirs ; and it seemed as if he was addressing
her. Perhaps he was, for often God's servants
unconsciously utter words which are a direct
message from Him to some particular soul.
The next day she came to see him, and after
that they often met in the huts of the poor,
and he sometimes came to St. Agathe. He,
too, watched her with interest. How could
it be otherwise ? D'Auban's affection for the
beautiful stranger was no secret to him, and

for his sake he tried to become better acquainted with her, to find out something of her past life, of her former associates, of her former place of residence. It was of no use. He was not more successful than D'Auban himself, or than Simonette. He did not express any suspicions, and yet he did not seem perfectly satisfied. He still advised him to be cautious.

'She looks so good! she is so good!' d'Auban would say.

'Well, so she does,' he would answer with a smile, 'and I hope she is so; but I wish she would tell us where she was born, and where and when M. de Moldau died. I have a fancy for facts and dates, baptismal and marriage certificates.'

Some months elapsed, and brought with them little outward change in the lives of the little band of emigrants. It was a monotonous existence, as far as the surface of things went; but it had its under-current of cares and interests, of hopes and fears.

'Men must work and women must weep'— such is the burthen of a popular song which has often been sung in luxurious drawing-rooms by men who do not work and women who seldom weep. But it was true of those dwellers in the wilderness whom chance had brought together, and who were beginning to care more for one another than those should do who are not looking forward to a time when, before God and men, they may be all in all to each other. She often wept; sometimes with passionaate grief, or, if others showed her affection, with a kind of child-like sorrow which shows a latent disposition to be comforted.

He worked very hard for her and for others also, for his was not a narrow selfish love. It widened his heart to all human sympathies. Perhaps there was a little self-interest in it too. To every person whose passage to the grave he smoothed, and who whispered with their last breath, ' I will pray for you in heaven,' he said, ' Pray for her.' To those who blest him for his kind-ness or his charity, he again said, ' Ask God to bless her.' And the blessing he desired for that beloved one was the gift of Faith. He thought he saw its dawning, and watched its progress with anxious hope. The winter came, and stillness was on the prairie—the stillness which is like that of a mist lying on a waveless sea. The snow was on the ground, the last brown and yellow leaves falling from the seared branches, and the mighty rushing of the neighbouring river, the only sound heard in the depths of the windless forest.

It was a picturesque group which sat round the blazing pine logs in the hall of the pavillon. Madame de Moldau was the centre of it. What a clever French girl said of a princess of our day might have applied to the lady of St. Agathe— '*C'est la réalité de l'idéal.*' Simonette's dark arch countenance, d'Auban's handsome sunburnt face, and M. de Chambelle's grey hairs, contrasted with her fair and radiant beauty. As a background to the principal figures of this picture sat Indian women nursing their children—men mending nets or feathering arrows. Negroes and whites and red men mixed together, crouching by the fire and enjoying the warmth. They were all devoted to Madame de Moldau since she had begun to take notice of them, and she liked them to come in and to surround her. As her spirits improved, she lost her love of solitude, and the homage of her dependants was evidently agreeable to her. She now seldom saw D'Auban in the morning, but was evidently not well pleased if he omitted to come in the evening. She avoided long or intimate conversations with him, but always listened with the greatest attention to what he said to others or in general conversation. None could see them together without perceiving that he was becoming devotedly attached to her—no one, at least, who felt any interest in watching the progress of this attachment. M. de Chambelle evidently rejoiced that he had found in him a fellow-worshipper, and the dark-eyed girl sitting at her feet knew perfectly well that every word Madame de Moldau uttered thrilled through Colonel d'Auban's heart. She knew also that her mistress watched for the sound of his footfall on the grass just as she did herself, and that when he was in the room there was a brightness in her face which passed away when he left it.

It was a singular bond of union between persons so different from each other, and in such different positions ; that they should be interested in the same person, though in a very dissimilar way. This sympathy was felt, though not acknowledged. If d'Auban wished something done, both were eager to carry out his plans. If he stayed away longer than usual from St. Agathe, both were depressed, and each knew what the other was thinking of. The grateful enthusiastic girl's affection was a kind of worship. The reserved and sensitive woman's regard—the highly-educated lady's feelings—were of a different nature. This was often evinced in the little daily occurrences of life. Once, when he was ill, Madame de Moldau would not believe that he was too ill to come to St. Agathe. Simonette turned pale at the thought of his doing so, for Father Maret had said it would be imprudent. Yet on another occasion, when a man was drowning, she was glad he plunged into the river to save him at the risk of his life, whilst Madame de Moldau entreated and commanded him to desist from the attempt. To see him honoured, admired, and beloved, was the passion of the young quadroon — to be cherished and cared for and petted by him, Madame de Moldau's principal object.

There was as much variety in the subjects talked of in those evenings at St. Agathe as in the appearance of the persons gathered together in that remote spot from the most opposite parts of the world. Tales were told and songs were sung which had called forth tears and smiles under other skies and amidst other scenes. Stories of the black forest and the Hartz mountains; legends of Brittany and of the bocage; traditions of the salt lakes and the fen-lands—of African tribes and slavery in Brazil—were told in prose and verse, wild and rude at times, but now and then full of the poetry which belongs to the infancy of nations. Father Maret was one day relating that a Frenchman had escaped death by promising the savages, if they would spare his life, that he would prove to them that he held them all in his heart— a pledge he redeemed by discovering a looking glass which he wore on his breast. There was a general laugh, and from Madame de Moldau's lips it came sweetly ringing like the chirping of a bird in a hedgerow. d'Auban had never heard her laugh; M. de Chambelle not for a very long time. Their eyes met, and there was a silent congratulation in that glance. The laugh which had gladdened their hearts was like the first note of the cuckoo on a spring-day, telling of green shoots and budding blossoms at hand.

On the same evening, when Father Maret was going away, Madame de Moldau followed him to the door, and said a few words to him. When she returned there was a very pensive expression in her countenance. Simonette was distributing some maple sugar to the labourers about to depart. They were as fond of it as children. M. de Chambelle was dozing. There was still some heat in the red embers, though the fire had nearly burnt out. Madame de Moldau stood by the chimney gazing on the fantastic shapes of the gleaming ashes. D'Auban said to her:

'I am so glad, madame, that you like Father Maret and see him often.'

She sighed deeply. 'How could one know and not like him, and not admire him? But . . . .'

'But what?'

'He is very severe.'

' In what way? '

Madame de Moldau coloured, and did not answer.

' Oh, that silence! that perpetual silence. Will you never have the least confidence in me. Do not you see, do you not feel how devotedly . . . . ? ' he was going to say, ' I love you,' but he was checked by a look, in which there was perhaps a little haughtiness. At least he fancied he saw something like pride in the sudden drawing up of her swan-like neck, and the troubled expression of her eyes ; but if so, it lasted but an instant. In an earnest feeling manner she said, ' If we are to be friends, dear M. d'Auban, and we certainly must be friends, and continue so, abstain, I beseech you, from appeals and reproaches, which give me more pain than you can imagine. I know how trying my silence must often be to you ; how often I must appear cold and ungrateful . . . . '

' No, no, indeed it is not that. On the contrary, it is your kindness which emboldened me to speak as I did just now.'

' One thing I will tell you which you will be glad to hear. I am thinking of becoming a Catholic.'

' Thank God for it,' he exclaimed.
' Madame, I have prayed and hoped for this
ever since I have known you.'

' *Have* you indeed prayed for it? You do
not know what it may involve; ' her voice
faltered a little.

' Sacrifices, perhaps?' he gently said, and
paused, hoping·she would say more. But
just then M. de Chambelle woke up and
made a thousand apologies for his drowsiness.
She seemed glad of the interruption, and
d'Auban went away.

As he walked home, he turned over in
his mind everything that had passed during
the last eighteen months since Madame de
Moldau's arrival. That lapse of time had
not thrown any light on the points which
from the first had puzzled him. A mystery
is never a pleasant thing—seldom a blessed
one. The trackless wilds of the New World
had already been polluted by many a foot
which had set its impress on the worn-out
surface of the Old World in characters of
blood. Many had brought with them ill-
gotten gains wherewith to traffic amidst new
scenes and new dupes. How many, also, to

hide a name once held up to public disgrace, and begin a new life, not of penitence and atonement, but of artifice and sin. He had never for a single moment supposed it possible that Madame de Moldau belonged to any of these classes of emigrants. She was one of those beings, so he fancied at least, with whom it is impossible to couple a thought of suspicion. He would sooner have doubted the evidence of his senses than have deemed her guilty and deceitful. But it did not seem equally out of the question that she might be the involuntary accomplice, or rather the victim of the sins of others. Nothing could exceed the precautions taken by her and her father to conceal even the outside of the letters they received. M. de Chambelle always watched for the arrival of the boat, and fetched away himself the parcels and letters directed to them. He had also noticed that she always looked · nervous when he brought a newspaper with him. The arrival of one was rather an event in the settlement, and he sometimes offered to read the contents aloud. On one occasion, when he was doing so, he happened to look up and perceived that Madame de Moldau seemed very much moved, and caught sight of Simonette's eyes fixed upon her with a scrutinising expression. He made some slight comments on the various topics alluded to in the number of the *Mercure de France*, which he had just read; but his observations elicited no answers. Mention had been made in it of the war in Germany; of Madame de Maintenon's death; of the illness of Louis XV.; of a fresh conspiracy against Peter the Great, and his son's flight from Russia; of the coronation of George I.; a great conflagration at Brussels, and a murder at Prague. He took the paper home with him. Simonette called early the next morning and begged the loan of it for her mistress.

' I was sure,' she said, ' that madame would ask to see it again; there is something in it which I know would particularly interest her.'

D'Auban felt greatly tempted to ask what it was she alluded to. Simonette had often of late showed a desire to talk to him of her mistress, especially in reference to the mystery in which her past life was shrouded; but he had always checked her. He had been the means of placing this girl with Madame de Moldau, and he would not on any account have availed himself of any information she might have acquired in order to discover her mistress's secrets. Seeing he made no reply to her observation, Simonette took the paper and went away.

All these circumstances made him anxious and thoughtful; one thing, however, gave him comfort. She who had been apparently drifting on life's sea like a rudderless bark, was now about to enter the haven. A prudent and tender hand would soon probe the wound so long and sedulously concealed. Hope and blessings were in that thought.

CHAPTER VI.

I thought to pass away before,
And yet alive I am . . .
A still small voice spake unto me
Thou art so full of misery:
Were it not better not to be?
A second voice was at my ear,
A little whisper silver clear,
A murmer ' be of better cheer.'
So heavenly toned that in that hour
From out my sullen heart a power,
Broke like the rainbow from the shower.

Tennyson.

But a more celestial brightness, a more ethereal beauty
Shone on her face and encircled her form when, after confession,
Homeward serenely she walked with God's benediction upon her.
When she had passed it seemed like the ceasing of exquisite music.

Longfellow.

A FEW days later d'Auban met Madame de Moldau coming out of the church of the mission. He saw her before she could see him. She seemed to be gazing with admiration on the scene before her. It was an afternoon of wintry but exquisite beauty. No transparent vapour, no mist laden with dew obscured the grand outlines or dimmed the delicate features of nature. The distant hills and the smallest blade of grass stood out in beautiful distinctness in the brilliancy of the sunshine. But as he drew near, and she still remained motionless and absorbed in contemplation, he felt that it was not the beauty of earth and sky that was filling her soul with extasy—not the brilliancy of the cloudless heavens which rivetted her upward gaze. He guessed, and rightly guessed, that she had that day laid at the foot of the cross the burthen so long borne in silence; that the poisoned arrow had been drawn from her breast. He was deeply moved; for he loved the woman who midway in his life had come to sadden by her silent sorrow, and yet to cheer by her gentle companionship, the loneliness of his exile. He longed to hear her say that she was one with him in faith, that henceforward they would worship at the same altar, that one great barrier between them was for ever removed. He spoke to her in a loud voice; she turned round and held out her hand to him.

'Yes,' she said, in answer to his question, 'it is as you suppose. I am a Catholic.'

For the first time since his mother had been laid in her quiet grave in the little churchyard of St. Anne, d'Auray, tears rose in his eyes.

'Blessed be this hour and this day,' he murmured, with uncontrollable emotion. 'It has made us one in faith. May not our hearts and our lives be also for ever united! Madame de Moldau, will you be my wife?'

The moment he had uttered the words he would have wished to recall them; for she looked beyond measure grieved and distressed. It had been an irresistible impulse. He did not feel sure that she was not angry. There was such a burning blush on her cheek, and such a singular expression in her countenance; but the blush passed away, and a look of great sweetness took the place of that strange expression.

'M. d'Auban,' she said, earnestly and steadily, 'it is better at once, this very day, under the shadow of the cross beneath which we stand, to tell you the truth.'

'Oh, yes!' he exclaimed; 'the truth—the whole truth.'

'The truth which what you said just now

compels me to speak. For every possible reason we can never be more than friends; and if you would not drive me away from the home, where after much suffering I have found peace, and if you would still help me to be good and happy, you will never allude to this subject again.'

'Is this an irrevocable decision ?'

'It is not a decision I have had to make ; it is, I repeat it, a truth I am telling you.'

'You are not free, then ?'

'No, I am not free.' She paused and hesitated a little. 'If I was so there would still be reasons why I could not be your wife.'

He remained silent. The disappointment was severe. She saw it was. Her voice trembled as she said—

'You have been all kindness to me, and the truest friend a woman ever had. I owe you more than I can ever repay. But do not ask me to explain ; if you can, banish the wish to know more about me than that I was once miserable and am now contented; —that I had neither faith or hope when I came here, and that now, thanks to you, I have both.'

'That is enough for me!' he eagerly cried —'quite, quite enough. I will seek to banish all other thoughts. The hope I had dared to indulge was not altogether a selfish one.'

'I know it well. You wanted to help, to comfort me. Now your friend knows all.' She said this, pointing to Father Maret's house. 'He has given me the consolation, the advice I so much needed. He is teaching me where to find strength ; he will direct my future course. But this I wish to say before I leave you to-day. Whether we are to continue to dwell in the same place, or should we part not to meet again, there is a thought that will never leave me as long as I live. I may forget many things—many there are I would fain forget but what you have done for me. . . .' She stopped, almost unable to speak for tears, and pointed to the part of the church where the altar stood, then almost immediately added, 'I never can forget that you brought me *here*; that you brought me to *Him*!'

It was not all at once that d'Auban could collect his thoughts sufficiently to realise fully what had passed that day, and how different had been the result from what he had expected. The event he had so ardently desired had indeed come to pass, and ardent also was the gratitude he felt for this great blessing; but the earthly hopes connected with it had suddenly vanished. What he had felt to be the great barrier between him and Madame de Moldau was removed, and yet was he to give up all idea of marrying her. 'Not free!' He repeated those words over and over again. 'Not free, and even if free, never to be his wife.' He pondered over the meaning of these words, and formed a thousand different suppositions in connexion with them. The mystery was to remain as deep as ever, he had all but promised not to try to discover it. A hard struggle it was, from that day forward, to conceal feelings which were stronger than he was aware of. During the whole of the past year he had looked forward to a time when he might avow them. He had formed projects and built up schemes connected with a vision of domestic happiness. When he used to read aloud to the assembled party at St. Agathe, or when he drove Madame de Moldau in his sledge over the noiseless frozen prairies, or when bringing home the game after a hunting expedition, he was always dreaming of the time when she would be his wife; and as the hue of health returned to her cheek, and elasticity to her step, as her laugh was now and then heard about the house and in the garden; and above all, when she began to attend the Church of the Mission, and to join in all its services, the dream turned into a real hope, the sudden overthrow of which was a bitter trial. Had she given him reason to hope? Had she encouraged him to love her? This is often a difficult question to answer, especially when people have been thrown together under extraordinary circumstances, or when affection may exist to a certain degree unconsciously. He dwelt on that last thought. He could not but think she cared for him, but then, if she was not free, their relative position was not only a difficult, but also a dangerous one, and perhaps she would be advised to leave St. Agathe, or perhaps he ought to go away himself. This would be scarcely possible, considering how his own and M. de Chambelle's fortunes were embarked in his present undertakings. He felt himself bound, and this was the practical resolution he formed, not to complicate the difficulties which might arise on this point by giving way henceforward to the expression of feelings not warranted by simple friendship. He would not, by word or look, recall to her mind the words he had hastily spoken, or give her reason to think that he cherished them in his breast—nay, he would try to subdue them. He would work, not seven years only, as the patriarch for his bride, but, if needs be, all his life, without hope or reward. It was a difficult resolution to act up to, but his sense of honour, his feelings of generosity as well as the dictates of conscience, the dread of driving her away from St. Agathe, enabled him to keep it. His strength of character and habits of self-control stood him in good stead. She did not guess how much he was suffering, whilst everything went on as usual in the course of their daily life.

Meanwhile, another conversion had taken place at St. Agathe. M. de Chambelle, a philosopher of the new school of French infidelity, a despiser of creeds, a free thinker,

who had taken unbelief on trust as some do
their belief; but who, if he worshipped
nothing else, worshipped Madame de Moldau
—began to feel leanings towards a religion
which made her look so much happier. He
borrowed a prayer book, went to church and
tried to say his prayers; and when he caught
the fever, and shivering, weak, and miserable,
was laid up for several weeks, Father Maret,
like a Jesuit that he was, sat up with him
night after night and robbed him of his scepticism. It oozed from him in the silence of
those watches whilst he lay suffering in his
uneasy bed, and Christian love and fatherly
kindness came near for the first time to his
aged heart. There was one green spot in
that poor withered heart, but it had never
been watered by the dew of heaven. Life
had never been much more than a ceremony
to him till it had become a suffering. He
had bowed and smiled and fidgetted through
its long course, and was puzzled at finding
what a weary thing it had become. But
when he recovered from this illness, the feeble
wistful face wore a happier look. The timid
heart and narrow mind expanded in the sunshine of faith.

A festival day was at hand at the Mission. It was to take place on the 8th of September, and great preparations were making for it both at St. Agathe and at the Concession d'Auban. Wreaths of flowers, large nosegays of roses and magnolias, and heaps of candles made of the pure green wax of the country, had been conveyed across the river on the preceding evening; and early in the morning, Madame de Moldau, Simonette, and Antoine joined Thérèse and her friends, and helped them to decorate the church. Beautiful were the bunches of feathers brought by the Christian Indians, and the skins of leopards and bisons which carpeted the floor of the sanctuary. Garlands of Spanish moss, intermixed with white and purple blossoms, hung from one pilaster to another on both sides of the church.

In the afternoon there was to be a feast for the children, and Simonette had prepared large bowls of sagamity sweetened with maple syrup, and baked cakes of Indian corn.

Great was the excitement of the youthful assembly, gay the scene, and happy the faces of the congregation, when, after mass, they spread themselves over the greensward and

began to play and eat under the tulip trees.
A French fiddler struck up the 'Carillon de
Dunquerque,' which set his country people,
old and young, dancing away with all their
hearts. The negroes' banjoes marked the ca-
dence of their characteristic melodies; whilst
the Indians accompanied with yells and
shrieks their pantomimic and, for the most
part, figurative performances.

Madame de Moldau had never witnessed
anything like this before. She was much
amused with the animated scene, and, throw-
ing down her straw hat on the grass, entered
into its spirit with the glee of a child. As
she was playing with a little negro boy, who
had jumped into her arms, her hair got un-
fastened and rolled down her back.

'Do call Simonette to put up my hair,'
she said, with a bright smile, to d'Auban,
who was standing a little way off.

He went to look for her. Thérèse said
she was gone to St. Agathe to get some provisions which had been left behind. He
walked towards the river and saw her coming. He saw, the minute he caught sight of

her face, that she was in one of her troubled moods.

'Madame de Moldau wants you,' he said.

'There are people at your house who want *you*, sir,' she answered.

'Have you been there?'

'No, but I saw their servant Hans at the pavilion. He says they have brought you letters.'

'Are they French?'

'They speak French, but I think they are Germans or Russians.'

'I must go and see about them. Will you tell Madame de Moldau that perhaps I may bring them to the village this afternoon? It will be an amusing sight for European travellers.'

'She must come home, sir. M. de Chambelle is worse again. He is gone to bed with the fever.'

'I am very sorry to hear it; and what a pity that it should be to-day. She seemed so happy—so amused!'

Simonette made one of her usual shrugs, and said, 'She had better make the best of her time, then.'

D'Auban thought her manner very dis-
agreeable, but he knew it always was so
when she was out of temper, and supposed
this was just now the case. Simonette went
on to the village, whilst he crossed the river,
and hastened first to St. Agathe, where he
found M. de Chambelle ill in bed, as Simonette had said, and somewhat light-headed
—and then to his own house, where he
found the three gentlemen she had mentioned.

He had never seen any of them before.
General Brockdorf was a stiff, military-looking
man, a Hanoverian by birth, but an officer in
the Russian army; M. Reinhart was also a
German, and Count Levacheff was a Russian.
He was by far the most pleasing of the
three. They had brought him letters of introduction from the Vicomte de Harlay, and
also from M. Perrier, at whose house they
had been staying during the days they had
spent at New Orleans. They were now
travelling to Canada through the Illinois and
the Arkansas.

After half an hour's conversation, he set
before them some refreshments, and, begging

them to excuse him for a short time, he hurried back to St. Agathe, to see if Madame de Moldau had returned. She was so shy of strangers, that he did not venture to bring these travellers to her house without her permission. She had just arrived with Simonette, who had rowed her across the river. He saw at once that she was very nervous.

'Some travellers are just arrived,' he said, as he joined them.

'So I hear,' she answered. 'Do they stay long?'

'No, only a few hours. Two of them are friends of De Harlay's. They would like very much to see his *folly*. Would you have any objection to my bringing them here?'

'Who and what are they?'

D'Auban mentioned their names, and added, 'I have heard of the two first, but I know nothing of M. Reinhart.'

'He was on board the boat which brought us up the river. I would rather not have seen him again. Have they told you any news?'

'Not much—nothing of importance; but

everything about the Old World is more or less interesting here.'

'Where do they come from?'

'From Paris, in the last instance.'

Madame de Moldau bit her lip, and pressed her hand on her forehead. She stood the picture of irresolution.

'It is very provoking that M. de Chambelle should be ill,' she said, 'and too ill even to advise me.'

The tone in which this was said would have pained d'Auban, if he had not at the same time observed that her eyes were filled with tears.

'There is really no necessity for your seeing these gentlemen,' he gently said. 'They need not come at all if it distresses you; or, if you like to stay upstairs, I could show them the hall and the verandah.'

'Oh! of course I know I can do as I like.'

This was said with a slight irritation of manner, which did not escape him. She seemed to have the greatest difficulty in making up her mind.

'You can bring them here,' she said at

last, but did not mention whether it was her intention to see them or not.

He supposed she meant to keep in her own apartment.

When he left the house she went up to her father's room. He was dozing, and talked in his sleep of missing volumes, and the binding of a book which had been sent by the King of Poland. She sighed deeply, gave some directions to his Indian nurse, and went to change her dress.

When she came down to the parlour she had put on a large lace veil, which nearly covered her face as well as her head. She called Simonette.

'Get the shawl,' she said, 'which we used to hang against the window. My eyes are weak; I should like the room darkened.'

This was done, and she sat down with her back to the light. Simonette was looking almost as nervous as her mistress. 'Here are the gentlemen,' she said, when the hall-door opened.

D'Auban almost started with surprise at finding her in the parlour, and at the darkness of the room. He introduced the strangers.

She greeted them with her usual graceful dignity of manner, and then said in a low muffled voice which did not sound like her own: 'I hope, gentlemen, you will excuse my receiving you in so dark a room. My health is not strong, and the light hurts my eyes.'

D'Auban thought of the way he had seen her a few hours before playing with the children in the broad sunshine, and a chilling sensation crept to his heart.

General Brockdorf made some complimentary remarks on the beauty of St. Agathe, and mentioned his acquaintance with M. de Harlay.

Count Levacheff, who had also seen him in Paris, playfully described the Frenchman's ecstasy at finding himself again in the capital of the civilised world. 'For my part,' he added, 'I find it very interesting to travel through a country so unlike what one has seen elsewhere. The grandeur of the scenery is sublime, and makes one forget the vulgar evils of insufficient provisions, tormenting insects, and rapacious boatmen. I suppose that the beauty of the country has lost its novelty, and perhaps its charm, for you, madame?'

'The views are beautiful and the climate also,' Madame de Moldau answered, in the same unnatural voice. Turning to General Brockdorf, she said: 'Is it for the sole pleasure of travelling that you visit this country?'

'Not altogether, madame. The Emperor of Russia has commissioned me to draw up a report of the natural features and peculiar productions of this newly discovered continent. Everything which tends to progress, to enlightenment, and to civilisation attracts the attention of his imperial majesty.'

'Is the Czar as active as ever,' asked d'Auban, 'in carrying out his vast designs?'

'He has achieved wonders,' the General replied, 'and only lives to plan yet greater marvels.'

'But are there not men of eminence and worth in Russia who, whilst they allow the merits of some of the Czar's innovations, do not approve of his mode of government, and who, whilst they admire the genius exhibited in the sudden creation of a new capital, have not transferred to it their attachment to the old Russian metropolis—time-honoured Moscow ?'

'You are right,' exclaimed Count Levacheff, 'the heart of Russia is in Moscow.'

'Not its brains,' said the General.

'That last-mentioned article,' observed Reinhart, who had not yet spoken, and who kept his eyes fixed on Madame de Moldau with marked pertinacity, ' the Czar chiefly imports from foreign countries. St. Petersburg is a haven of refuge for needy Frenchmen and German adventurers. The Czarovitch has announced his intention of sweeping away, when he comes to the throne, the invading hordes, as he calls them. He is a genuine Moscovite.'

'He is as great a brute as ever lived,' said Levacheff.

' With the exception of his father,' observed d'Auban, who even at that distance of time could not quite endure to hear the Emperor mentioned with praise.

'Ah! but there is this difference between them,' said the Count: 'genius and strength adorn the character of the father with a kind of wild grandeur. The weakness of the son makes his brutality as despicable as it is hateful.'

'Is it true that he has lately returned to Russia upon Count Mentzchikoff's assurance that he would receive a full pardon?'

'He has certainly returned, but has been thrown into prison. His friends say he was cruelly deceived. Others, that some fresh plots were discovered since that promise was given. What gave much surprise in Russia was his taking refuge at the Emperor of Austria's court, seeing the reports which were circulated at the time of his wife's death.'

'Was he supposed to have had a share in her death?'

'So it was said. People believe she died in consequence of a violent blow he had given her. Others said her attendants poisoned her at his instigation.'

'Aye,' put in Reinhart, 'and ran away with her jewels.'

'The matter was hushed up. It was thought the Prince would have been implicated in the matter, and the Czar did not at that time wish to come to extremities with him. Now it is thought he would be glad to crush him. The late princess was a great favourite of his, and he was very angry with his son for the horrible way in which he treated her, as well as for his intrigues with the reactionary party. The Czarovitch is devoted to the old Moscovite cause, and fanatically attached to the orthodox religion. But the politics of Russia are not, I should imagine, the most interesting subject of conversation to a French lady, who would no doubt prefer to hear of the gaieties of Paris, never more brilliant than last winter.'

M. Reinhart moved his chair nearer to Madame de Moldau's, and, interrupting Count Levacheff, said, 'I fancy that madame is better acquainted with St. Petersburg than with Paris. If I am not mistaken, she has resided there some years?'

Simonette turned crimson. Her hand was resting on the back of her mistress's chair, and she felt her trembling violently.

She answered, however, with tolerable composure: 'I have been both at Paris and at St. Petersburg.'

D'Auban's heart beat fast when she said this. He had never heard her say as much as that before about her past life.

'Did not madame occupy a position in the household of the late princess?'

'No, sir,' answered Madame de Moldau in a louder and more distinct tone of voice than before; then slightly changing her position, she turned to Count Levacheff and said, 'How was the Empress Catherine when you left St. Petersburg?'

'In good health, I believe,' he answered.

'You said, I think, the Czarovitch was returned?'

'Yes, and he was imprisoned in his palace.'

'Did you hear anything of his son?'

'He lives in the Emperor's palace.'

'Is he like his grandfather?'

'More like his late mother, I believe.'

'I saw the young prince two or three times whilst I was at St. Petersburg; but I am not apt to take much notice of children, even when they are imperial highnesses. He seemed a rosy little boy; with fair curling hair.'

Madame de Moldau sank back in her chair, apparently exhausted with the attempt she had made at conversation. D'Auban proposed to conduct the visitors over the plantation. But she made an effort to sit up, and again addressed Count Levacheff.

'Was the Comtesse de Konigsmark at St. Petersburg?' she asked.

Before he had time to reply, M. Reinhart said in a half-whisper, 'Would not you like to obtain some information, madame, about a casket which was once in the countess's care?'

Madame de Moldau fainted away. Simonette received her into her arms, but there was no tenderness in the expression of her face as she bent over her drooping form; she looked on her colourless face with more scorn than pity. D'Auban felt angry and miserable. He led the strangers out of the house into the garden, and murmured something to the effect that Madame de Moldau was a great invalid.

'If you take my advice,' said Reinhart, 'you will have as little as possible to do with that lady. I feel certain now of what I suspected at New Orleans.'

'What do you mean?' exclaimed d'Auban fiercely.

He would willingly have thrown into the river or trampled under foot the being who dared to speak of Madame de Moldau in that insulting manner; but, at the same time, a sickening doubt stole into his heart.

Reinhart was so struck by his agitation, that it suddenly occurred to him that discretion is the best part of valour. He had not the slightest wish to entangle himself in a quarrel with Madame de Moldau's friend, who might be, for aught he knew, a lover, or even an accomplice. He therefore said, with a forced smile, 'The explanation is a very simple one: from what I have heard of this lady's beauty and charm, and what I have seen myself to-day, I should think there would be great danger of a man's losing his heart to her.'

It was impossible not to accept this explanation, and equally so to believe in its veracity. The conversation dropped. Meanwhile Alexander Levacheff had disappeared. As he was leaving the house, he had turned back, as if by an irresistible impulse, and returned to the parlour. The door was open, the window also. Madame de Moldau's veil had fallen off her face. The light was shining on her pale, lovely features. Simonette hastened to the door, and closed it almost in his face. He stood in the hall apparently transfixed — motionless with astonishment. Then, sinking down on a bench, hid his face in his hands, and remained buried in thought. D'Auban, engrossed and agitated by Reinhart's remarks, had not at first noticed his absence. When he did so, and proposed to return for him, General Brockdorf objected that they had no time to spare; that Levacheff did not know a turnip from a potato, or a sugar-cane from a coffee-plant, and would be only too thankful to have been left behind.

When Madame de Moldau had recovered a little, she went upstairs to M. de Chambelle's room. Levacheff saw her go by, but she did not notice him. After she had passed, he pressed his hands on his eyes, like a man who tries to rouse himself from a dream.

She had seated herself by her father's bed and dismissed his attendant. He was asleep. His aged features looked thin and sharp, and his scanty grey hairs were matted with perspiration. She rested her head against the bed-post, and faintly ejaculated, 'Faithful unto death! Faithful through a strange, long trial; and now at last going to leave me. Oh patient and devoted heart! am I indeed about to lose you? Ah! if you had not been lying here helpless and unconscious, I should not have seen those men! Why did I see them? It was rash—it was imprudent. I do not know how to take care of myself. It would have been better to have died. Oh no! God forgive me! what am I saying? I know—I know, my God, what mercies you had in store for me. You are good—goodness itself; but I am very weak.' She heard voices in the garden, and went to close the window that the sick man might not be disturbed. It was d'Auban and his companions going away. Gradually the sound of footsteps receded. Simonette knocked at the door and gave her a slip of paper, on which some German words were written. White as a marble statue, trembling and irresolute, she stood with it in her hand, gazing on the writing as if to gain time before she answered.

'Where is the gentleman who gave you this paper?'

'In the entrance-hall.'

'Where are the others?'

'They have walked out with M. d'Auban.'

'Show him into my sitting-room; I will see him there.'

In about an hour d'Auban and his two companions returned. As he entered the house he said to Simonette, who was standing in the porch talking to Reinhart's servant:

'How is your mistress?'

'Oh, pretty well, sir!' she answered in a careless tone.

'Is she upstairs?'

'She went upstairs, sir, when you went out.'

'Do you know where Count Levacheff is?'

She turned away without answering.

Provoked at her uncivil manner, he sternly repeated his question.

She seemed to hesitate a little, and then said:

'I am not sure, sir, if madame wishes it known that he is with her in her private room.'

At that moment, through the thin partition-wall which divided the hall from the little sitting-room, d'Auban heard Madame de Moldau speaking in her natural voice, and in a loud and eager manner. These words reached his ears:

'You promise, Count Levacheff, that you will not tell any person on earth that you have seen me?'

'Madame, if you insist upon it, I must; but do think better of it. Let me stay, or return, or at least write——'

D'Auban tore himself away, and ordered Simonette to go away also. She obeyed, but shrugged her shoulders, and said:

'It does not matter now whether I listen or not, M. d'Auban; I know all about her.'

It was in an almost mechanical manner

that d'Auban performed the remaining duties
of hospitality towards the travellers. When
Levacheff joined them in the verandah it
would have been difficult to say which of the
two seemed most disinclined to conversation,
most absorbed in his own thoughts. General
Brockdorf's unceasing flow of small talk
proved a great resource during the last half
hour of their stay. At last it was time for
them to go. D'Auban could not bring himself so much as to mention Madame de
Moldau's name in their presence; yet, when
they got into their boat and moved away
from the shore, he sighed, as if feeling that
he had lost the last chance of clearing away
his doubts. Levacheff and Reinhart evidently
knew much more about her than he did.
For two days he stayed away from St.
Agathe; on the third he was sent for. M.
de Chambelle was much worse, and wished
to see him. Father Maret had also been
summoned, but had not yet arrived. He
hastened to the pavilion. The sick man's
couch had been carried into the parlour,
where there was more air than upstairs.
Madame de Moldau was sitting by his side.

He was in a high fever, talking a great deal, and much excited. When d'Auban came in he cried out :

'Ah ! M. d'Auban, I was afraid I should die without seeing you. Why have you stayed so long away ? '

' I have been very busy about the plantations,' he evasively answered.

Madame de Moldau tried to move away, but she could not disengage her hand from her father's dying grasp.

' M. d'Auban,' cried the sick man in a feeble querulous voice, ' you must make me a promise before I die. Without it I cannot die in peace ; all that Father Maret can say is of no use. You know I am a young Christian though an old man. Will you promise to do what I ask you ? '

' Anything in my power I will do, my dear friend, to meet your wishes,' d'Auban kindly answered.

' Will you, then, promise me never to leave her—to take care of her as I have done ? '

Madame de Moldau hastily bent over the old man, and said, ' Dear good father, you are asking what cannot be.'

'Why not? why not?' exclaimed M. de Chambelle, raising himself in the bed; 'it is my only hope, my only comfort. I tell you, I cannot, and I will not die, and I will not listen to what Father Maret says about submitting to God's will, if he does not promise me this. You will be alone in the world; not one friend left; more lonely than a beggar in the streets. That cannot be God's will. Some days ago I dreamed that he whom we never speak of had sent a man to kill you. I don't think it was a dream. I heard strange voices in the house—I am sure I did. If he sends him again, who will take care of you if M. d'Auban does not?'

'Oh! for heaven's sake, dear father, be quiet, do not talk.'

'No, I will not be quiet—I will not be silent—I must say what is in my heart. When I went to confession I told Father Maret I hated somebody; I did not say who it was. Do not try to stop me. I have always obeyed you——'

'Oh, do not say that!' exclaimed Madame de Moldau, wringing her hands.

'But I must speak now; I must plead

your cause before I die. Oh, Colonel d'Auban! will you forsake her?' He grasped her hand so tightly that she could not extricate it, and fixed his eyes with a wild expression on d'Auban's face. 'Look at her,' he cried; 'look at her well. She ought to have sat upon a throne, and men bowed down before her; and now for so long she has only had me to wait upon her——'

Madame de Moldau sank down on her knees by the bedside, pressed to her lips the hand which clasped her own, and exclaimed, 'Oh, more than father! patient, kind, and loving friend! be silent now. Grieve not the heart you have so often comforted. Listen to your daughter, who would have died had it not been for you. Had God taken you from me when first we landed on these shores, I must have perished. Then, indeed, you would have had reason to fear for me. It is different now. Let this thought comfort you. Carry it with you to a better world. I have a friend who will never forsake me.'

M. de Chambelle turned his dying eyes on d'Auban, who stooped and whispered, 'She is not speaking of me. God is her friend now.'

'Yes, dear father, I have a home in His church, a father in His priest, friends and brethren in the household of the faith. The words of the Bible, " Thou shalt no longer be called the forsaken one," apply to me, once an outcast and a wanderer on the face of the earth.'

'Thou shalt no longer be called the forsaken one!' ejaculated the old man, gazing upon her with an enquiring look, as if trying to realise the meaning of the sentence. Still he turned to d'Auban, and, drawing him nearer to himself, whispered in his ear :

' Will you not stay with her?'

' If she will let me, I will,' he answered in the same low voice.

' Oh, thank God for that!'

' And wherever she goes, please God, I will watch over her.'

' Oh! now I feel the good God has heard the prayer of a poor old sinner, who never did any good in his life. Where is Monsieur l'Abbé? The last time he came I would not say I was ready to die if it was God's will.

You see, I was in waiting ; there was nobody to take my place ; the second librarian used to do so sometimes long ago.   I wonder if he is dead ; I am sure he has not forgotten her——'

Madame de Moldau hid her face in her hands ; there was no checking the old man's rambling, and he detained d'Auban in the same way as he detained her.   He was silent for two or three minutes, then, starting up, he turned towards him in an excited manner.

' You know I never said you were to marry her.   That would be a *mésalliance*.   What would they say at the palace ? '

The blood rushed into d'Auban's face ; but he said in a calm and steady voice, without looking at Madame de Moldau, ' His mind is beginning to wander.   He does not know what he says.'

After awhile M. de Chambelle fell asleep. By the time he woke again Father Maret had arrived. He remained with him awhile alone, and then administered to him the last Sacraments.   Extreme unction was followed, as it so often is, not only by increased peace and tranquillity of soul, but by some bodily improvement.   In the afternoon he appeared to rally considerably; still d'Auban did not venture to leave the pavilion, for he was continually asking for him. When the sun was setting and a deep tranquillity reigned in the house, in which everybody moved with a light step and spoke under their breath, he sat in the porch with Madame de Moldau, conversing on the interests of the Mission and the condition of the poorer emigrants, and carefully avoiding any allusion to the past or the future, or the recent visit of the European travellers. The soft westerly wind, laden with perfumed emanations—the rustle of the leaves, and the murmuring voice of the streamlet hurrying towards the river, like one feeble soul into eternity—the singing in parts of some German labourers at work in the neighbouring forest—the beauty of the sunset sky, of the green turf and the distant view—breathed peace and tranquillity. These soothing sights and sounds were hardly in accordance with the sorrowful and anxious thoughts which filled their minds. Father Maret was walking up and down the glade saying his office. When he closed his book his kind and pensive glance rested on those two dwellers in the wilderness, the secrets of whose hearts he was acquainted with, whose future struggles and sufferings he foresaw. The hours went by on their noiseless wings, and death hovered over that pretty fanciful St. Agathe, which seemed more fitting to harbour a tribe of fairies than the sorrowing and the dying. As the light waned, M. de Chambelle grew weaker. The prayers for a departing soul were read over the expiring form of one who at the eleventh hour had been received into the fold. The priest held the crucifix before his dimmed and failing eyes. He gazed upon it earnestly, and then on Madame de Moldau. It was no longer to human friendship he was committing her. He made a sign that he wished to speak to her once more. She bent over him, and he found strength to whisper, ' I have at last forgiven him.' One more look at her, and one at the crucifix, and then the old man died; and she whom he had loved so long and well lifted up her voice and wept, at first almost inaudibly, then, as the full sense of her loss, the terror of her desolate fate, broke upon her, a loud and bitter cry burst from her lips. My child! my sister! When the heart is wrung by some great grief, when a blow falls on a closed but not seared wound, there is always a cry of this sort. The old man weeping by the grave of his child remembers the wife of his youth. The bereaved mother in her hour of anguish calls on her own departed mother. The condemned criminal thinks of the priest who taught him his catechism. The past comes back upon us in those first hours of overwhelming sorrow and self-pity as if the grave gave up its dead to haunt or to console us.

The two kind friends by her side did not try to check the mourner's tears. One of them looked gently upon her, like a compassionate angel to whom God reveals the secret ways by which He trains a soul for heaven. The other gazed on her bowed-down form with the yearning wish to take her to his heart and cherish her as his own; but he scarcely dared to utter the words of sympathy which rose to his lips, lest they should be misunderstood. His mind was in a dark and confused state. New thoughts were working in it. Thérèse came to pray for the dead and to comfort the living. Simonette was, as usual, active in doing everything needful, but there was more displeasure than sorrow in her face; and once, when she saw d'Auban looking at Madame de Moldau with an expression of anxious tenderness, her brow darkened and an impatient exclamation escaped her lips.

The funeral was simply performed, and the European stranger buried in the little cemetery, where many a wanderer from the Old World rested by the side of his Indian brethren in the faith. Many an offering of fresh-gathered flowers was laid on his grave, for both settlers and natives had become attached to the kind childlike old man, and pitied his daughter's bereavement.

CHAPTER VII.

*   *   *   *   *
See what a ready tongue suspicion hath.   *Shakespeare.*

Moreover something is or seems
That touches me with mystic gleams,
Like glimpses of forgotten dreams.   *Tennyson.*

By Father Maret's advice Madame de Moldau came to spend a few days with Thérèse. Her hut was clean though a very poor abode, and the change of air and scene proved beneficial to her health. The near neighbourhood of the church was a great comfort also, and to get away from Simonette a relief. Her temper had grown almost unbearable, and her manner to her mistress very offensive. She governed her household and directed all her affairs, however, with so much zeal and intelligence that she could ill have spared her; but the momentary separation seemed at this time acceptable to both.

D'Auban came sometimes to the village to see Madame de Moldau; but since the stranger's visit, and especially since what had passed when they both watched by M. de Chambelle's death-bed, they had not felt at their ease together. He especially felt exceedingly embarrassed in his intercourse with her. It now seemed to him evident that she must have occupied some position which she was intensely anxious to conceal. The promise he had heard her exact from Count Levacheff and poor M. de Chambelle's rambling expressions about a *mésalliance* and a palace pointed to this conclusion. He racked his brains to form some guess, some supposition as to the possible cause of her retirement from the world and the mystery in which it was enveloped. Once it occurred to him that, with the romantic sentimentality ascribed to some of her countrywomen, she had, perhaps, sacrificed herself, and abandoned a lover or even a husband for the sake of some other person, and resolved never to make her existence known. It was just possible that a highly - wrought sensibility, a false generosity unchecked by fixed religious principles, might have led her into some such course, and involved her in endless difficulties. It was not difficult to believe she was of noble birth. Nobility was stamped on her features, her figure, and every one of her movements. It struck even the Indians. They said she ought to be a Woman-Sun—the title given to the female sovereigns of some of their tribes. During her stay with Thérèse, Madame de Moldau improved her knowledge of the language of the country, and under her guidance occupied herself with works of charity. At the end of a fortnight she returned to St. Agathe. D'Auban was waiting for her with his boat at the spot they called the ferry. He saw she had been weeping, and his heart ached for her. It was a desolate thing to come back to a home where neither relative or friend, only servants, awaited her return. He made some remark of this kind as they approached the house.

'Yes,' she said, sinking down on the bench in the porch with a look of deep despondency —'yes, the return is sad. What will the departure be?'

D'Auban started as if he had been shot. 'What do you mean? You are not going away?'

'Yes, I must go, and you must not ask me to stay.'

He did not utter a word, but remained with his eyes fixed on the ground, and his lips tightly compressed. She was distressed at his silence, and at last said :

'You are not angry with me, M. d'Auban, for resolving to do what is right?'

'Right!' he bitterly exclaimed. 'Alas! madame, can I know what is right? I know not who you are, where you come from, where you are going. What I do know is, that from the first day I saw you my only thought has been to shield you from suffering, to guard you from danger, to watch over you as a father or as a brother. When you told me to give up other hopes, I shut up my grief in my heart. I never allowed a word to escape from my lips which could offend or displease you. What more could a man do? Have I ever given you reason to distrust me? Have I obliged you to go away? But I am a fool; what poor M. de

Chambelle said has misled me. You have
other friends, I suppose, other prospects———'

'None.'

'Then why—why must you go? What
has been my fault? Cannot you forget my
rash words? Cannot you rely on my promise
never again——'

'Oh, M. d'Auban! it is not your fault that
I must go. It was not your fault that I heard
you say what I can never forget. Mine has
been the fault. Would that the suffering
might be mine alone ; because your sympathy
at first, and then as time went on your friendship, was precious to me ; because I thought
only of myself, and of the consolation I found
in your society, sorrow has come upon us
both. Nay, I will add one word more.
Before I became a Catholic it did not seem
to me quite impossible. . . . my ideas were
different from what they now are. . . . I did
not consider myself absolutely bound. . . .
Now, you see, there remains nothing for us
but to part.'

'Why should you think so? Why not let
me work for you—watch over you? . . . You
can trust me.'

A deep blush rose in her cheek, as she quickly answered, 'But I cannot—I ought not to trust myself.'

A strange feeling of mingled pain and joy thrilled through his heart, for he now felt that his affection was returned; but he also saw that what she had said was true—that they must part. Another silence ensued; then, with a despairing resignation, he asked, 'And where can you go?'

'To Canada,' she answered. 'Father Maret will recommend me to the Bishop of Montreal and to some French ladies there.'

'Will you sell this property?'

'No; not if you will manage it for me.'

'Yes, I will; and the day may come when you will revisit it.'

'Perhaps so,' she said, with a mournful smile—'when we are both very old.'

'And how will you travel?'

'There is a party of missionaries expected here, and a French gentleman and his wife. They are on their way to Canada. Father Maret is going to arrange about my joining them. He hopes we may reach Montreal before the wet season sets in.'

'So be it,' murmured d'Auban; and from that moment they both sought to cheer and encourage each other, to bear with courage the approaching separation. With true delicacy of feeling she showed him how entirely she confided all her interests to his care—how she reposed on the thought of his disinterested and active friendship. He planned for the comfort of her journey, and resolved to spare her as much as possible the knowledge of what he suffered. In spite of the reserve she observed as to the past and the sad uncertainty of the future, they understood each other better than they had done yet, and there was some consolation in that feeling.

But when he had taken leave of her that day, and he thought that he should soon see her go forth with strangers from that house where he had so carefully watched over her, his courage almost failed. The sight of the blooming garden, the brightness of the sunshine, oppressed his soul; and when the sound of a light French carol struck on his ear he turned round and angrily addressed Simonette, who was watering the flowers in the verandah and singing at the same time.

'I am surprised to see you in such good spirits so soon after your kind old master's death, and at the very moment of his daughter's return to her desolate home. I thought there was more gratitude in your character.'

The expression of her face changed at once. 'Do *you* call me ungrateful, M. d'Auban?' she said, with a sigh. 'Well, be it so. Even that I will put up with from you. But what gratitude do I owe to these people?'

'They are your benefactors.'

'Indeed! Is that the meaning of the word in Europe? Is the person who devotes her time, her labour, and her wits to the service of poor helpless beings, who can do nothing for themselves, and receives a little money and perhaps a few kind words in return, the obliged party, and they the benefactors? In this country, I think, the terms might be reversed.'

D'Auban felt even more provoked with her manner than her words, and answered with a frown—

'I wonder that you can speak of your mistress in this manner.'

'My mistress! I have never considered her as such. I undertook this hateful service, M. d'Auban, solely at your request and for your sake, and you call me ungrateful. You speak unkindly to me, who have worked hard for these people because you wished it, and that your will has always been a law to me. For your sake, and in a way you do not know and do not understand, I have suffered the most cruel anxiety. Because I have been afraid of your displeasure I have been silent when perhaps I ought to have spoken; and yet for your sake I ought to speak, and, at the risk of making you angry, I will. Yes, at all risks, I must say it. You are blind—you are infatuated about that woman——'

'Hush! I will not hear such language as this.'

'But you must hear it, or I will expose her to those who will listen to the truth. Others shall hear me if you will not.'

'Speak then,' said d'Auban sternly. The time had arrived when he felt himself justified in listening to Simonette's disclosures. Matters had come to a crisis, and on Madame de Moldau's own account it was necessary he should hear what Simonette had to say. He made a sign to her to sit down, and stood before her with his arms folded and looking so stern that she began to tremble. 'Speak,' he again said, with more vehemence than before, for he saw she hesitated.

At last she steadied her voice and spoke as follows : ' Sir, it was at New Orleans that I first saw Madame de Moldau. I heard at that time that there was something mysterious about her. People said she was not called by her real name, and a servant, who arrived there with her, and soon after returned to Europe, let fall some hints that she had reasons for concealing her own. She and her father came on board our boat at night ; M. Reinhart, and his servant Hans, were amongst the passengers. He said he had seen her before, and that there were strange stories about them—that they were supposed to be adventurers, or even swindlers. Nobody could understand why an old man and a handsome delicate woman, not apparently in any want of money, should come to this country with the intention of taking up their abode in a remote settlement. At Fort St. Louis M. Reinhart and Hans left us, and I did not see them again till they came here with those other gentlemen. When you proposed to me to enter Madame de Moldau's service you must, I am sure, remember that I declined to do so. I only wish I had persevered in my refusal. But you seemed very anxious I should accept your offer. You said it would be an act of charity. You did not speak of benefactors then. My father urged me also. But what really decided me was this: It was said you admired her, and that you would soon marry the lady at St. Agathe. I thought if I lived with her I should be sure to find out whether the stories about her were true or false, and that I might be the means of saving you from marrying an impostor——'

'You have no right to speak in that way,' interrupted d'Auban, tried beyond endurance by the girl's language and manner. 'It is a vile calumny.'

'It is no such thing, M. d'Auban ; you desired me to speak and you must hear me to the end. I know she does not seem an impostor—I can hardly believe her to be one ; but you shall judge yourself. Well might people wonder where their money came from ! I soon found out that she had many rich jewels in her possession. One of the things Hans had told me was, that her father had sold some valuable diamonds at New Orleans, and lodged the money in a banker's hand. It was reported at the same time that, in a palace in Europe, a casket was stolen which contained the jewels of a princess lately dead. It must have been the princess mentioned in the newspaper you were reading out loud one night some days ago, and which madame sent me to borrow from you the next morning. Well, the report was that her servants had stolen this casket and fled the country.'

'St. Petersburg was the town you mean, and the princess, the wife of the Czarovitch of Russia.'

'Yes, the Princess Charlotte, I think they called her. Hans says his master is persuaded that these people are those very servants.'

'I don't believe a word of it.'

'He says that M. de Chambelle's real name
is Sasse, and that he lived at the court of the
princess's father; that he saw him there a
great many years ago. And now I must tell
you what I myself discovered. I picked up
on the grass near the house a casket with a
picture inside it set in diamonds, and on the
back of the casket, in small pearls, was
written the name of Peter the First, Emperor
of all the Russias. I saw it with my own
eyes, and the diamonds were very large, and
the gold beautifully worked. I have seen
things of this sort at New Orleans, but
nothing half so handsome.'

'You saw this with your own eyes!' repeated d'Auban, turning very pale. 'But
are you certain it belonged to Madame de
Moldau?' he quickly added. 'What did
you do with it?'

'I was almost inclined to take it to you,
sir, or to Father Maret; but on the whole
thought it best to return it to her.'

'And when you did so?'

'She seemed embarrassed, but said it was
her property. And I made some observations which were painful to her, about people

having secrets; and she spoke of parting with me. But it did not come to that. She did not really wish me to go, nor did I really wish to leave her. I have never been happy since that time. Sometimes I cannot help feeling sorry for her; but when I think she is deceiving you, I should like to drag her before the governor and accuse her to her face. When those gentlemen came here, Hans told me that the story of the stolen jewels was talked of more than ever at New Orleans, and people now say that the princess was murdered, that her husband was concerned in it, and had himself helped the servants to escape. Did you not notice that M. Reinhart asked her that day if she had been in the princess's household? She answered, " No ;" but I could feel, as I held the back of her chair, that she trembled, and when he spoke of the casket, then she fainted right away. Good heavens! how ill you look, M. d'Auban! Alas! alas! what can I do? I am only speaking the truth. I wish with all my heart it was otherwise. Hate me if you will—despise, disbelieve me, but do not be rash. Do not marry this deceitful woman. You suspect me, perhaps. You think that I hope or expect . . . Oh never, never in my wildest dreams has such a thought crossed my mind! If she was as good as she looks, if she would make you happy, willingly would I be her slave and yours all my life. If you knew how wretched it makes me to see you look so miserable! But, oh! if you marry her and she is guilty!——'

'My dear Simonette,' said d'Auban, interrupting her, but speaking much more gently than he had yet done, 'I am sure you mean kindly by me. I should be indeed ungrateful did I not believe in your sincerity. The circumstances you have related are most extraordinary; I certainly cannot at this moment account for them. But still, I would entreat you to suspend your judgment. Do not decide against her till you know more.'

'Ah! that is what Father Maret always says; but I am afraid she deceives you both.'

D'Auban eagerly caught at those words. 'Is that what he says? Then *he* does not think her guilty?'

' He does not say one thing or the other.'

' Well, Simonette, I again thank you for your kindness to myself, and I entreat you, for the present, at least, not to speak on this subject to anyone else. I feel bound to tell you that, in spite of the apparent evidence to the contrary, I still firmly believe in Madame de Moldau's innocence.'

' And you will marry her ?' exclaimed Simonette, wringing her hands.

D'Auban tried to speak calmly, but he felt as if the secret recesses of his heart were being probed by the poor girl's pertinacious solicitude.

' There is not the least prospect of my marrying Madame de Moldau. Do not distress yourself on that point ; and for my sake be kind and attentive to her during the time she will yet remain here.'

' Is she going away, sir ? '

D'Auban covered his face with his hands. She looked at him with anguish. ' How you must hate me ! ' she murmured.

' No,' he said, recovering his composure. ' No, Simonette, much as I suffer, I do not blame you, my poor girl. It is natural you should have had suspicions—it could not have been otherwise. But I cannot talk to you any more now; I must be alone and think over what you have told me. May we all do what is right. If you are going to the village this evening, tell Father Maret I will call on him early to-morrow, and ask him and Thérèse to pray for us.'

That evening he sat in his study gazing on the glowing embers and absorbed in thought. Sometimes he started up and walked up and down the room, making a full stop now and then, or, going up to the chimney, rested his head on his hands. 'It would be too strange—too incredible,' he ejaculated; 'and yet the more I think of it, the more does the idea gain upon me. No, no; it is a trick of the imagination. If it was so, how did I never come to think of it before? Yet it tallies with all the rest. It would explain everything. But I think I am going out of my mind to suppose such a thing.'

There was a knock at the door, and when he said 'Come in,' Simon appeared.

He had returned, he said, from the north

lakes, whither he had accompanied the travellers who had lately been d'Auban's guests. He thought he would like to hear of their having journeyed so far in safety. Hans had come back with him; he had had a dispute with his master about wages, and they had parted company. 'He is gone to St. Agathe this evening; I fancy he admires my girl. They have always plenty to say to each other. He is a sharp fellow, Hans, and does not let the grass grow under his feet.'

D'Auban felt a vague uneasiness at hearing of this man's return. It was from him Simonette had heard all the stories against Madame de Moldau. 'I should not think,' he said, 'that this man can be a desirable acquaintance for your daughter.'

'He seems a good fellow enough, and says that if she will take his advice he can show her how to better herself.'

'In what way?'

'He does not exactly say, but I don't see why she should leave her present situation. Her wages are good, and I do not find she has anything to complain of; but she has always had a queer sort of temper. For my part,

I think she might go farther and fare worse.
Well, M. d'Auban, I only just looked in to
let you know about your friends; I am off
again to-morrow to the Arkansas. Have
you any commands?'

'No, thank you, nothing this time. But
just stop a minute; you have not had a glass
of my French brandy. What do you know
of this Hans's former history?'

'Not much. He has been in Spain, and
Italy, and Russia. We never do know much
of the people who come out here.'

'I think you had better warn Simonette
not to act on his advice as regards a change
of situation. He cannot be a safe adviser or
companion for her.'

'She does not like him a bit. The girl's
as proud as a peacock; I wish she was
married and off my hands. Well, this *is*
good cognac, M. d'Auban. It does a man's
heart good, and puts him in mind of *la
belle France*. I was thinking, as I walked
here, how good your brandy always is.'

' It was fortunate, then, I did not forget to
offer you a glass of it,' d'Auban said with a
smile.

When the bargeman was gone he began
again to turn over in his mind the new strange
thought which had occupied him for the last
two or three hours. From the first day he
had made Madame de Moldau's acquaintance
he had been haunted by a fancy that he had
seen her before, that her face was not new to
him. But that afternoon, whilst Simonette
was talking to him, when she mentioned the
wife of the Czarovitch (the Princess Charlotte
of Brunswick), the thought darted through
his mind that the person she reminded him of
was this very princess. This idea brought
with it a whole train of recollections. Some
seven or eight years ago he was travelling
with General Lefort, and they had stopped
for two days at Wolfenbuttel, and been invited
to a dinner and a ball at the ducal palace. Now
that he came to think of it, what an asto-
nishing likeness there was between the lady
at St. Agathe and the Czarovitch's affianced
bride as he remembered her in her girlhood,
—a fair creature, delicate as a harebell, and
white as a snowdrop. But it was impossible.
He laughed at himself for giving a serious
thought to so preposterous a conjecture, for

was it not well known that that princess was dead? Had she not been carried in state to her escutcheoned tomb,

With knightly plumes and banners all waving in the
  wind,

and her broken heart laid to rest under a monumental stone as hard as her fate and as silent as her misery? Can the grave give up its dead? Had she returned from the threshold of another world? Such things have been heard of. Truth is sometimes more extraordinary than fiction. He thought of the story of Romeo and Juliet, and of the young Ginevra rescued from the charnel-house by her Florentine lover. It is impossible to describe the state of excitement in which he spent that night—now convinced that his conjecture was a reality, now scouting it as an absurdity—sometimes wishing it might prove true, sometimes hoping it might turn out false; for if the chivalry and romance of his nature made him long to see the woman he loved at once cleared from the least suspicion, and to pay that homage to her as a princess which he had instinctively rendered to the daughter of an obscure emigrant; on

the other hand, if she was the Princess
Charlotte of Brunswick, she was also the
wedded wife of the Czarovitch, and he saw
the full meaning of the words she had said on
the day she had been received into a Church
in which the holy band of marriage is never
unloosed, where neither ill-usage, nor deser-
tion, nor crime, nor separation, annihilates the
vow once uttered before the altar. Though
an ocean may roll its ceaseless tides and a
lifetime its revolving years between those it
has united, the Catholic Church never
sanctions the severance of that tie, but still
reiterates the warning of John the Baptist
to a guilty king, and that of Pope Clement
VII., fifteen hundred years later, to a licen-
tious monarch, ' It is not lawful; it may
not be.'

Of one thing he felt certain. If Madame
de Moldau was the Princess Charlotte, it was
impossible to conceive a more extraordinary
or more interesting position than hers, or one
more fitted to command a disinterested alle-
giance and unselfish devotion from the man
she had honoured with her friendship. If
something so incredible could be true, every

mystery would be explained—every doubt would be solved. The blood rushed to his face as he thought of the proposal of marriage he had made to one of so exalted a rank, and of the feelings which it must have awakened in her breast. 'Perhaps,' he thought to himself, 'though too generous to resent it, she may have found in those words spoken in ignorance one of the bitterest and most humiliating evidences of her fallen position;' but then he remembered the tacit avowal Madame de Moldau had made of feelings which did not imply that she was indifferent to his attachment. 'Ah!' he again thought, 'she may wish to withdraw not only from the man she may not wed, but from him whose presumptuous attachment was an unconscious insult! But I am mad, quite mad,' he would exclaim, 'to be reasoning on so absurd an hypothesis, to be building a whole tissue of conjectures on an utter impossibility; but then M. de Chambelle's dying words recurred to him—those strange incoherent expressions about a *mésalliance* and a palace, and their relations together, so unlike those of a father and a child, and yet so full of devotion on his side and of gratitude on hers.

One by one he went over all the circumstances Simonette had related. The reports at New Orleans, the sale of the jewels, the Czar's picture in her possession, the stranger's visit, her agitation when the casket was mentioned—everything tallied with his wild guess. It would have been evident had it not been incredible. As it was, he felt utterly bewildered.

As soon as light dawned he rode to the village. There he heard that Hans had gone away in the night with a party of *coureurs des bois*. He breakfasted with Father Maret, and all the time was wondering if, supposing Madame de Moldau was the princess, he was aware of it. She said she had told him everything about herself, so he supposed he did. This thought inspired him with a sort of embarrassment, and, though longing to speak of what his mind was full of, he did not mention her name. As soon as the meal was over he returned to St. Agathe, where he had business to transact with Madame de Moldau. He found her sitting at a table in the verandah looking over the map of the concession. She raised her eyes, so full in their blue depths of a soft and dreamy beauty, to greet him as he approached, and he felt sure at that moment that they were the eyes of the royal maiden of seventeen years of age with whom he had danced one night in her father's palace. He sat down by her as usual, and they began talking of business; but he was, for the first time perhaps in his life, absent and inattentive to the subject before him. He was reverting to one of those trifling circumstances which remain impressed on a person's memory, and which just then came back into his mind. When the young princess was dancing with him she had mentioned that the lady opposite to them had undergone a painful operation to improve the beauty of her features. 'I do not think it was worth while,' she said; and then, pointing to a mole on her own arm, had added— 'I have been sometimes advised to have this mole burnt off, but I never would.'

He remembered as well as possible where that mole was—a little higher than the wrist, between the hand and the elbow of the left arm. Could he but see the arm, which was resting near him on the table covered by a lace sleeve, all doubt would be at an end. He could not take his eyes off it, and watched her hand which was taking pencil notes of what he was saying. At that moment a small spider crept out of a bunch of flowers on to the table, and then towards the sleeve so anxiously watched. D'Auban noticed its progress with the same anxiety with which Robert Bruce must have observed that of the insect whose perseverance decided his own. The creature passed from the lace edging to the white arm. Madame de Moldau gave a little scream and pulled up the sleeve. D'Auban removed the insect, and saw the mole in the very spot where he remembered it. He carried away the spider and laid it on the grass. His heart was beating like the pendulum of a clock; he did not understand a word she was saying. He could only look at her with speechless emotion.

'Sit down again, M. d'Auban,' she said, 'and explain to me where you want to build those huts.'

He hesitated, made as if he was going to do as she desired, but, suddenly sinking down on one knee by her side, he took her hand and raised it with the deepest respect to his lips. She turned round, surprised at this action, and she saw that his eyes were full of tears.

'What has happened?—what is the matter?' she exclaimed.

'Nothing, Princess, only I know everything now. Forgive, forget the past, and allow me henceforward to be your servant.'

'You! my servant! God forbid! But, good heavens! who has told you? M. d'Auban, I had promised never to reveal this secret.'

'You have kept your promise, Princess; nothing but accidental circumstances have made it known to me. Do not look so scared. What have you to fear?'

'Oh! if you knew what a strange feeling it is to be known, to be addressed in that old way again. It agitates me, and yet—there is a sweetness in it. But how did you discover this incredible fact?'

'It is a long story, Princess. I saw you

some years ago at Wolfenbuttel; but it is only since yesterday that I have connected that recollection with the impression I have had all along that we were not meeting for the first time here.'

'Have you indeed had that feeling, M. d'Auban? So have I; but I thought it must be fancy. Did we meet in Russia?'

'No; I left St. Petersburg before your Imperial Highness arrived there. It was at the Palace of Wolfenbuttel that I saw you, a few months before your marriage. I was there with General Lefort.'

'Is it possible! I feel as if I was dreaming. Is it really I who am talking of my own self and of my former name, and as quietly as if it was a matter of course? But how extraordinary it is that you should have suddenly recollected where you had seen me! What led to it?'

'Simonette's suspicions about some jewels, and a picture in your possession.'

'Oh yes. I believe the poor girl thinks I have stolen them. I perceived that some time ago. I have been very careless in leaving such things about. I do not see any

way of explaining to her how I came by them;
but as I am going soon, it does not signify
so much.'

'Do you still think you must go, Princess? Does not my knowledge of what you
are alter our relative positions. If, imploring at your feet forgiveness for the past, I
promise——'

'Oh, kindest and best of friends, believe
me when I say, that it is the wedded wife,
not the Imperial Highness who feels herself
obliged to forego what has been a blessing,
but what might become a temptation. In
your conduct there has been nothing but
goodness and generosity. Would I could
say the same of mine. My only excuse is
that my destiny was so unexampled that I
deemed myself bound by no ordinary rules.
I fancied neither God nor man would call
me to account for its driftless course. I
should have let you know at once that
there were reasons of every sort why we
could never be anything more than friends to
each other. In those days I never looked
into my own heart, or into the future at all.
Bewildered by the peculiarity of my fate, I

felt as if every tie was broken, every link with the past at an end, save the only one which can never be dissolved—a mother's love for her child. I applied to myself the words of the Bible, " Free amongst the dead ; " for I had passed through the portals of the grave. It seemed to me as if I had survived my former self, and that ties and duties were buried in the grave on which my name is inscribed. I lived in a state that can hardly be conceived. It was like groping amongst shadows. Nothing seemed real in or around me. You raised me from that death-like despondency, that cold and silent despair. You made me understand that it was worth while to live and to struggle.'

She paused as if to collect her thoughts, and then said with a melancholy smile :

'Then you know who I am ? '

' Yes, Princess ; and in that knowledge there is both sadness and joy.'

' I ought to have told you long ago that I was married.'

" Forgive me, Princess, for having dared——'

' I have nothing to forgive. On the contrary, my gratitude for what you have done for me is too deep, too vast, for words. I do not know how to express it. You showed me there could be happiness in the world, even for me. And then you taught me by your example, still more than by your words, that there is something better and higher than earthly happiness. You made me believe in the religion which bids me part from you, and which gives me the strength to do so.'

'Thank God that we have met and not met in vain,' d'Auban answered, with the deepest feeling. 'Thank God for the sufferings of a separation more bitter than death, if we do but meet at last where the wicked cease from troubling——'

'Ay, and where the weary are at rest. But now, even now, I *am* at rest,' she added with an expression of wonderful sweetness, 'almost for the first time of my life; and though when I go from hence and leave you and Father Maret behind, I shall be the most lonely, perhaps, of all God's creatures, the most solitary being that ever wandered on the face of the earth seeking a spot wherein to hide and die, I feel happy——Can you understand this, M. d'Auban?'

'Yes; for it is the Christian's secret.'

'But you have always had faith—you cannot perhaps quite conceive the feelings of those who once were blind and now see. You don't know what it is to have lived half a lifetime in darkness, and then to feel the glorious light breaking in upon your soul and flooding it with sunshine!'

D'Auban was too much moved to speak for awhile, and then said, 'Would it agitate or pain you, Princess, to relate to me the particulars of——'

'Of my extraordinary history—my unparalleled escape? No, I think I can go through it, and I should like to do so. I wish you to know all that has happened to me. It will be a comfort to us hereafter to have spoken quite openly to each other before we parted.'

It was in the following words that Madame de Moldau told her story.

CHAPTER VIII.

MADAME DE MOLDAU'S STORY.

I will relate all my years in the bitterness of my soul.
Ezekiah's Song.

> And she hath wandered long and far
> Beneath the light of sun and star,
> Hath roamed in trouble and in grief,
> Driven forward like a withered leaf,
> Yea, like a ship at random blown
> To distant places and unknown.   *Wordsworth.*

'My childhood went by like a pleasant dream. The ducal palace in which I was born, with its gay parterres, its green bowers, and the undulating hills which surround it, often rises before me like a vision of fairy-land. My sister and myself were brought up like birds in a gilded cage, and with about as much knowledge of the external world as the doves we kept to play with or the gold-fish in our mimic lakes. Our governess was an elderly lady of rank, who had all the

kindness, the placidity, and the romantic
sentimentality of the Northern German
character. We were, I suppose, sweet-tem-
pered children, and scarcely a ripple marred
the smooth surface of our even days. Nothing but gentleness was shown to us. Study
was made interesting. We led a charmed
existence, such as is depicted in fairy tales,
and seeing nothing as it really is. We
thought peasants were like the shepherds
and shepherdesses made of Dresden China,
and that the poor were people who lived in
small houses covered with roses and called
cottages. As to the world of politics and
fashion, we formed our ideas of it from
Mdlle. de Scudéry's novels. Nothing vicious
or unrefined was suffered to approach us.
We were taught music and morality, languages and universal benevolence. Religion
was exhibited to us as a sentiment well
fitted to impart elevation to the mind, and
to give a relish for the beauties of nature.
Virtue, we were assured, was its own reward.
Oh! M. d'Auban, how well all this sounded
in the morning of life, in an atmosphere of
unruffled tranquillity and youthful enjoyment,

in those secluded bowers where my young
sister and myself wandered hand in hand,
playing in the sunshine, slumbering in the
shade, and resting our heads at night on the
same pillow.   The happiness of those early
years looked and felt so like virtue. And as
we grew older, the love of poetry and art,
and our intense affection for each other, and
our enthusiasm for the Fatherland and its
legends and traditions, filled up a space left
purposely vacant in our hearts and minds.
No definite faith was instilled into our souls.
We were instructed in the philosophy which
looks on all dogmas with indifference. It
was only on the map that we were permitted
to distinguish between the creeds which men
profess. We were to be educated to respect
them all, and to believe in none till the day
when diplomacy decided our fate, and our
consequent adherence to one religion or
another. Trained in indifference, doomed to
hypocrisy! None of those who surrounded
us held nobler views or a higher language
than this. That dear kind old friend, who died
the other day, you must have noticed yourself
the tone of his mind when first you knew

him. He was our chamberlain from the time we were old enough to have a household appointed for us. Even in those days we playfully called him father, as I have done in sad and sober earnest and with good reason since. But I will not linger any longer over the remembrance of those scenes and of that time. I will not describe to you Wolfenbuttel, the miniature valley, the smooth green hills, the silvery river, the old palace, the library where we used to see learned men assembling from all parts of the world——'

'I have seen it,' said d'Auban. 'I have seen those hills, that palace. I saw you and and your fair sister, the very day (so I was told at the time) that you were about to part with her.'

'Did you? It was the day after a ball.'

'Yes, that very ball where I was permitted to dance with you.'

'Ah! is it not strange that those who are destined to play so great a part in one another's life can be so unconsciously breathing the same air, gazing on the same scenes, speaking careless words to each other!——

But tell me, did you feel sorry for me then? Did you foresee what I should suffer?'

'I remember musing on the fate which awaited you, but with more of wonder than pity. It seemed to me as if the most savage of men must soften towards you, and I felt more inclined to compassionate those you were about to leave than to foresee suffering in a destiny which promised to be brilliant.'

'Well, I parted with my sister, took a last farewell of the happy scenes of my childhood, received a wreath of flowers at the hands of the maidens of Wolfenbuttel, and many a splendid gift from kings and from princes. I left the ducal palace and the fair valley in which it stands with a sorrowful but not a desponding heart, for I was fulfilling a woman's and a princess's part. Forgetting my father's house, I said to myself, going forth like Rebekah to meet an unknown husband in a strange land. My sister, so said the poets of the ducal court, was to wed the Austrian eagle; I was to be the mate of the Imperial bird of the north. "Joy to the Czarovitch's bride!" the sound rang in my ears, and my heart beat with more of hope than of fear. The title of the son of the Czar pleased my girlish fancy, and I had a romantic admiration for the great Emperor whom the philosophers and the men of letters of my country extolled as the greatest hero of the age. It was to Torgau that my father took me to meet Peter the Great and his son. I have often wondered if he had a presentiment that day of the doom of his child. I stood by his side in the chamber which had been fitted up for the first interview. The door was thrown open, and the Czar came in. I knelt at his feet and besought him to be a father to me. He spoke kindly to me. I raised my eyes to his face. It is a handsome one, as you know, but I was struck with the dead coldness of his eye, and the fearful twitch which sometimes convulsed his features. And then he presented the prince to me.'

Madame de Moldau paused, hid her face in her hands, whilst tears fell like rain through her slender fingers.

'It is too much for you,' exclaimed d'Auban, 'too painful, too agitating to go through

such a narrative—to speak of that man who
was——'

'Who *is* my husband—the father of my
child—my persecutor, my enemy, and yet
——Oh! sometimes, since I have had time to
look back upon the past, since in profound
self-abasement I have sunk at our Lord's feet
and felt my own need of mercy, I have
pitied *him*, and felt that others will have to
answer for much of his guilt. Yes, that great
man, his father, has dealt cruelly with a
nature that was not altogether bad. He cut
down the wheat with the tares in a heart as
full of wild passions and as fierce as his own,
but of a far different stamp. It is impossible
to imagine two beings brought up in a more
different manner than the Czarovitch and
myself. Darkness and gloom had over-
shadowed his cradle; the rancour which was
fostered in his soul from the earliest dawn of
reason was joined to a passionate attachment
to the customs, manners, religion, and language of the Muscovite nation. Early in life
he had felt a burning resentment at the
banishment and disgrace of his unhappy
mother, the Empress Eudoxia. In the visits

he obliged me to pay to " Sister Helen," the pale wild-looking recluse of the monastic prison of Isdal, I saw that the same passions which influenced him were eating her heart away in that horrible solitude ; and what a fatal effect they had upon his character! Yet I was glad ; yes, it was a relief to see that he loved her, that he loved anyone.   His detestation of the Empress Catherine was as vehement as his sense of his mother's wrongs.'

' There is something very fearful,' d'Auban said, ' in a child's hatred.   It is almost always founded on a secret or acknowledged consciousness of injustice, on the feeling that some great injury has been done to itself or to another.   Nothing destroys so effectually youthfulness of heart.'

' And the prince's hatred extended also in some measure to his father : he looked upon him as an oppressor whose will it was all but hopeless to withstand, but a sort of infatuation urged him on to the unequal struggle. There was not one subject on which the son did not abhor his father's policy. He detested foreign manners and foreign languages, and, above all, foreign innovations. He loathed the sight of the new capital, which had risen up in a day, and taken the place of the beautiful city of his birth—the Queen of the old Muscovite empire. The Emperor's assumption of supremacy in ecclesiastical matters, and the suppression of the patriarchate, were in his eyes acts of audacious impiety. His attachment to theological studies in his youth was a singular trait in his character. He had twice written out the whole of the Bible in his own hand, and was by no means an unlearned man. But at the time of our marriage he was surrounded alternately by his drunken companions and by the clergy of the Russian Church. From a child he was taught to conspire, and urged to carry on a fruitless contest with a master mind and a despotic will which crushed him and raised him up again with contemptuous ease. He was always lifting up his arm against the giant who despised him. Defeated, but not subdued, he maddened in the conflict, and vented his rage on those within his reach. M. d'Auban, do you remember the Indian legend that Thérèse repeated to us on the eve of New Year's Day?'

'The story of Hiawatha? I noticed at the time that some parts of it seemed to strike you very much.'

'It made me think of the struggle I am speaking of. Those stanzas particularly which describe how Hiawatha fought with his father, the ruler of the west wind, to avenge the wrongs of his mother, the lily of the prairie, the beautiful Wenonah. How he hurled at the giant the fragments of jutting rocks:

> For his heart was hot within him,
> Like a living coal his heart was;
> But the ruler of the west wind
> Blew the fragments backward from him
> With the breathing of his nostrils,
> With the tempest of his anger.

Yes, those words made me think of the Czarovitch's struggle against his iron-hearted father, who never loved him, but bore with him; and with a great patience, in which there was not one atom of feeling or of kindness, sought to make him a fit successor to his throne.

'Now, M. d'Auban, you can imagine with what feelings that rebellious spirit, that resentful son, that wild and weak young man, must have looked upon the bride which his father had chosen for him—the German bride, who could not speak one word of the Russian language, and who, with childlike imprudence, showed her aversion to many of the customs of Russia, some of them the very ones which Alexis would almost have died to uphold; who spoke with enthusiasm of the Czar; who babbled, God forgive her! of philosophy and free thinking, but loathed the sight of his vices and excesses. In those first days of marriage, of complete ignorance of all that surrounded me, how I rushed, like a fool, where angels, as the English poet said, would have feared to tread! How I unconsciously sported with the elements of future misery, and thought I could tame, by playful looks and words, the fierce nature of my husband!

' It was a few days after we had arrived at the palace at St. Petersburg, that I received my first lesson in the Greek religion ; and in the evening, whilst conversing with General Apraxin, I laughed at the pains which my instructor had taken to explain to me that the Czar could not be Antichrist, as the

number 666 was not to be found in his name.
I saw my husband's eyes fixed upon me with
a look of hatred which curdled the blood in
my veins. Another time I was listening
with a smile to the ridiculous account which
one of the Czar's favourite French officers
was giving of the discipline to which the
Russian peasants subjected their wives, and
of the pride which a true Muscovite woman
took in the chastisements inflicted by her
lord and master. The word " Barbarians "
escaped my lips. The Czarovitch started up
in a fury, and dealing me a heavy blow, exclaimed—" This will teach you, madame, to
turn into ridicule the ancient customs of this
nation."

'I turned away from him with a cry of
terror, and from that day I never was free
from fear in his presence. When the Czar
was within reach I felt sure of his protection,
but he was seldom at St. Petersburg or at
Moscow for any length of time, and I was
left to the tender mercies of my husband.

'Oh what that life was; what that life became—every part of it, every moment of it!
I had not one human being about me whom

I could trust, except my faithful M. de Sasse
—M. de Chambelle, as we called him here—
who alone had been suffered to accompany
me to Russia. He was of Russian parentage
himself, and obtained permission to enter my
household. The Countess of Konigsmark was
very kind to me, and there was one other
person in that great empire who also felt for
the Czarovitch's wife; one whom many speak
against; one whose life has been as extraordinary, though a very different one from
mine; one who may have been guilty towards others, God only knows, but to me a
friend to more than royal friendship true.
Never, as long as life and memory last, can I
forget the kindness of the Empress Catherine.

'The first day I saw her—it was just after
the Czar had recognised her as his wife—my
heart was very sore. Disenchantment, that
sickness of the soul—a still more hopeless
one than that of hope deferred—had come
over me. No one had said a word of tenderness to me since I had left my home. The
Countess of Konigsmark was not yet in
Russia. I had no feeling for or against the
new empress. My husband detested her;

but I had espoused none of his hatreds, and was more inclined towards those whom his friends opposed than those whom they favoured. When I saw her handsome face beaming upon me with the sunshiny look which, it is said, made her fortune, it seemed as if a ray of real sunshine had, for a moment, shone upon me. I suppose I must have looked very miserable. She had not yet learnt the cold reserve which royalty enforces. The womanly heart of the Lithuanian peasant warmed towards the desolate princess; she clasped me to her breast, and I felt hot tears falling on my brow. She doubtless guessed what I had already suffered, and the doom that was reserved to me; for she knew what it was to be wedded to a Romanoff —to live in fear and trembling with a hand on the lion's mane. She knew how fierce a thing was even the love of one of that race: well might she divine what their hatred must be. Our meetings were not frequent—our interviews short. The Czar, as you know, was ever travelling in and beyond his vast empire, and she was ever by his side. It was his desire, at that time, that the

Czarovitch should try his hand at governing during those absences. He took care, however, to restrain his power, and to have a close watch kept over his actions. He compelled me, in spite of the ever-increasing bad treatment of the prince, to remain with him; for he knew that all my ideas coincided with his own, and were opposed to those of my husband. He hoped I should gain an influence over him. It was a vain hope.

'I will not dwell on one circumstance of my history — which, as you have resided in Russia, you probably are acquainted with. You doubtless heard it said, that Charlotte of Brunswick had a rival in the person of a Russian slave.'

'I knew it,' said d'Auban, with emotion.

'It was no secret,' Madame de Moldau went on to say. 'The prince used, in my presence, to complain that the Czar had married a peasant, and that he had been compelled to wed a princess.

'Now you can understand what a fatal effect my position had upon me, as regarded religion. How I hated the creed which it had been agreed upon as a condition of my marriage that I should profess; which they wished to teach me, as if it had been a language and a science. A Protestant may be a sceptic, and yet scarcely conscious of hypocrisy in calling himself a Christian; but the Greek religion enforces observances which are a mockery if practised without faith in them. I would not receive the sacraments of the Greek Church. The Czar did not compel me to it; but many a fearful scene I had with my husband on that account. When, on state occasions, I went to church with him, my presence only irritated his fanaticism. His religion consisted in a kind of gloomy, intense devotion to a national form of worship, identified with his prejudices, but without any influence on his heart or life. My own early impressions were too vague, too indefinite, to offer any standing-ground between the tenets which were forced upon me and the scepticism in which I took refuge. Can you wonder that I became almost an infidel?'

'It would have been strange had it been otherwise,' d'Auban answered. 'It is a great mercy that the principle of faith was not utterly destroyed in your soul. But it is, thank God, only wilful resistance to truth which hopelessly hardens the heart. You were guiltless of that.'

'Everything that now appears to me in another light, under another aspect, was then distorted, as if to delude me. The prince used to take me in secret to the monastery of Isdal to see his mother and his aunt, the Princess Sophia—the so-called nuns, the unhappy recluses whose bodies were confined in this cloistered prison, whose hearts and minds were incessantly bent on ambitious projects, on intrigue and on revenge. Sister Helen's fierce denunciations of the Czar and the Empress Catherine still ring in my ears. When I am ill and weak, her face, as I used to see it, half concealed by a dark cowl, haunts me like a spectre. And the Czar's sister—her haughty silence—her commanding form — her eye bright and cold as a turquoise, watching the foreigner with a keenness which froze the blood in my veins; how I trembled when I encountered its gaze! how I shuddered when Sister Helen called me, daughter!

'I am afraid of wearying you, M. d'Auban, with the detail of my sufferings, but I want you to know what my life has been——'

'I would not lose one word, one single word, of this mournful story. It tells upon me more deeply than you think. Go on. It will be better for you to have told, and for me to have heard, that such things have happened in God's world. May He forgive those who have thus wrought with you, my——'

He stopped. The words 'beloved one,' were on his lips, but were checked in time. It was a hard task for that man to hear her tale of sorrow, and not pour forth in burning words the feelings of his heart.

She continued: 'Everything was a trial to me during those dreadful years. The barbarous magnificence of the court, which always in the absence, and sometimes in the presence, of the Czar was mixed up with drunken orgies and savage revelries, which sometimes, out of caprice, the prince forced me to witness. At other times I was left in absolute neglect, and even penury.

'You have sometimes wondered at my

patient endurance for a few weeks of the horrors, as you termed them, of Simon's barge, and the hut where we were first sheltered under these sunny skies. You did not know that I had once almost starved in a cold northern palace, well-nigh perished from neglect.

' At a moment's notice, a summons would come to accompany the prince to meet his father at some distant part of the empire; five or six hundred leagues were to be traversed, day and night, with scarcely any interval of repose. He detested those forced marches, and used sometimes to feign illness in order to avoid them. When we joined the court I was secure for awhile from ill-treatment, for the Czar was always kind, the Empress affectionate to me ; but then I used to suffer in another way. You will understand it : something you said to me about the Czar makes me sure you will. Since my girlish days I had looked upon him with admiration — his prowess, his intellect, his energy, the immense works he had achieved, his gigantic creations, had stimulated all the enthusiasm of my nature. Perhaps my husband would not have hated me so bitterly if I had not exalted his father's name, his schemes, and his innovations with an enthusiasm, and in a way, which was gall and wormwood to him. When I was suffering the deepest humiliations, when insulted and ill-used by the Czarovitch, I used to glory that I was the Czar's daughter—that my child would be his grandson. But shadows gradually darkened these visions. A cold chill was thrown over my youthful anticipations. This did not arise from the stories my husband and his friends related against the Emperor. I disbelieved them. The slaughter of thousands of men—the extermination of the Strelitz—I recked not of. The majesty of the crown had to be vindicated. The young Czar, in the hour of his might and of his triumph, bore the aspect of an avenging divinity in my blinded vision, and the glories of a nation rose out of the stern retributive justice of these acts.

'But when in his palace, for the first time, I saw him give way to passion, not as a sovereign, but as a savage (you used that word once; I fear it is the true one);

when I saw him, with my own eyes, strike his courtiers; when with trembling horror I heard of his cutting off the head of a criminal with his own hand, and another time of his administering the knout himself to a slave— then the veil fell from my eyes—then the dream was over. The disgusting buffooneries he delighted in were also a torment to me. The cynical derisive pantomimes enacted in his presence, in which even the sacred ceremony of marriage was profaned and ridiculed; the priesthood, degraded though they might be, turned into ridicule—it was all so revolting, so debasing. No doubt he was great in what he conceived and in what he executed. No doubt he created an empire in a few years, and raised up cities and fleets even as other men put up a tent or launch a ship. But, M. d'Auban, do you believe that he has founded that empire on a lasting foundation—do you think that the examples he gave will bequeath to the Russian nation those principles of morality which are the strength of a people?'

'I place no reliance,' answered d'Auban, 'in reforms brought about by despotic power, or in a civilisation which improves the intellect and softens the manners without amending the heart and converting the soul. Did you ever venture to express these ideas to the Czar?'

'Sometimes, in a general way, but you must remember, that whatever may have been right in my impressions at that time, was the result of a conscientious instinct, not of any definite principles. I was afraid of showing him how much I disliked the bad taste of his favourite amusements. Once when the Czar had given way before me to a degrading transport of passion, he said to me afterwards, "Ah, it is easier to reform an empire than to reform oneself." There was something grand in this acknowledgment from one with whom no one on earth would have dared to find fault.'

'Amendment would have been grander. But the fact is, he had no wish to amend. He has no faith, no principles. Ambition is his ruling passion, and what in him looks like virtue is the far-sighted policy of a wise legislator. What unmitigated suffering the atmosphere of that court must have been to a

nature like yours! The natural goodness of
your heart, as well as your refined tastes
incessantly offended by the iniquities which
compassed you about on every side, and at
that time, no firm footing on which to take
your own stand in the midst of all that
corruption.'

'Yes, even those whom I had a better
opinion of, and who took an interest in me,
men embued with the philosophical ideas
which are gaining ground so fast in
France and in Germany, but who scorned
the grosser vices and coarse manners of my
husband's companions, had nothing better to
recommend to me, in order to strengthen my
mind and guard me against temptation, than
reading Plutarch's Lives and Montesquieu's
works. General Apraxin, Count Gagarin, and
Mentzchikoff, the Emperor's favourite, were
of the number of these friends who ridiculed
the longbeards, as they called the clergy, and
applauded my aversion to the ceremonies of
the national religion. They opened my eyes
to the dangers which surrounded me. One
of them informed me that every lady in my
household was a spy—some in the Emperor's

and some in my husband's interest. Another warned me never to speak in a low voice to any of my attendants, as I should be suspected of conspiring. And one day the Countess of Konigsmark (this was about two years after my marriage) brought me secretly a box containing a powerful antidote against poison, with the assurance that I might have occasion to use it; that there was no longer any doubt that the Czarovitch intended to make away with me, in order to marry the slave Afrosina. Then fear of another sort became my daily lot; uneasiness by day and terror by night. If ever the story of Damocles was realised in a living being's existence, it was in mine. The torment of that continual fear became almost unbearable, and the home-sickness preyed upon my spirits with unremitting intensity. It was at once the prisoner's and the exile's yearning—the burthen of royalty and that of poverty also. I was penniless amidst splendour; in debt, and deprived, at times, of the most common comforts of life. On state occasions decked out with eastern magnificence, at home in miserable penury. Often I was obliged to submit to arrangements which were intolerable to a person of even ordinary refinement. In the temporary residences which we occupied during the progresses of the court, my apartment was crowded with female slaves, both by day and by night; and there was more vermin in some of the Muscovite palaces than in the wigwams of our poor Indians.

' One of the peculiarities of my fate in those days was that of being, in one sense, never alone, and continually so in another. If amongst my attendants I seemed to distinguish one from the rest—if any affection seemed to spring up between one of my ladies and myself, she was at once dismissed from my sight, exiled to Siberia, or compelled, perhaps, to marry some person of obscure station.'

' An equally dreadful fate in your eyes, princess,' said d'Auban, in a voice in which there was a slight shade of wounded feeling. Madame de Moldau did not seem to notice it.

' The loss was the same to me in both cases,' she said. ' The severity of the trial to them must have depended on the peculiarities of their own character, or the disposition of

the person they were forced to wed. I
envied them all, I believe—the exiles to
Siberia most. I would have gone anywhere,
done anything to fly away and be at rest;
and there was no rest—think of that! no
rest to body, heart, or mind! One while the
Czarovitch would bring his friends into my
room, and hold his drunken revels there,
playing at a game where the penalty consisted in swallowing large bowls of brandy at
one draught. He used roughly to compel
me to join in these sports, and brutally re-
sented my ill-concealed disgust. Another
while he assembled some of the Greek priests
of the old school, and held with them long
theological discussions in my presence. If I
looked weary and distracted he called me a
German infidel, and cursed the day he had
married me. Now you see why I shuddered
when you first spoke to me of religion. It
was as if the spectre of past suffering had
suddenly risen up before me, and touched me
with its cold hand. One more word before
I arrive at the closing scene of these long
years of anguish. I have been a mother, but
I have not known a mother's joy. I went

through the trying hour of a woman's life, without one word of affection or of tenderness to soothe or to support me. In a cold desolate apartment in the winter palace, more like a hall than a chamber, my son was born. The Czar and the Empress were hundreds of leagues away. There was a ceremonial to be observed which was as the laws of the Medes and Persians. No particle of it was to be infringed, but the actors in it forgot or refused to come and perform their parts; and no peasant, no slave, no criminal, was ever left in such helpless abandonment as the Czarovitch's wife. They carried away my infant. They kept him out of my sight. They left me alone shivering, shuddering, pining in solitude, conjuring up visions of terror during the long interminable nights, and nervous fancies without end. Hating to live, fearing to die, trembling at every sound, weary, weary unto death, I lay there thinking of my child in the hands of strangers, deeming that the poison I had been threatened with might be even then destined for him, and the while cannons were firing, and bells ringing, and men carousing for joy that an heir was born to the house of Romanoff. Forty days elapsed and I was at last permitted to see my son. The Czar had returned, and the Empress Catherine brought him in her arms to my bed-side. . . . I looked at the little face a long time. She was very patient with me (the Empress), she did not try to stop my weeping. She laid the baby one moment on my bosom, but it was not to stay with its mother. The Czar would not allow his son the possession of the heir to the throne. I was allowed to see him sometimes, not often. That same day I was churched in my bed-chamber, in the presence of the Emperor and the Empress. The Patriarch performed the ceremony. I went through it with a heart of stone. There was no thanksgiving on my lips, and no gratitude in my heart. I felt as if I was an atheist, and wished myself dead.'

'Are you very tired?' anxiously asked d'Auban, frightened at Madame de Moldau's paleness, as she leant back in her chair, and closed her eyes for a moment.

'No; I was thinking of the visits I used to pay to my child at stated times only.

How I used to stand by the cradle, covered with ermine, gazing on my sleeping baby, and how when he awoke he turned away crying at the sight of a stranger—of his mother. And on my return to my detested home, what wild dreams I had of escape, of freedom! What vain schemes would flit at those times across my fevered brain of a flight to my own land with my infant in my arms, of hiding in some lone wood, amidst the green hills of my native land, where for one hour I might sit with my child upon my knees, gazing into his eyes. I have heard you pity the slave whose child is sold from her bosom. Alas! I was almost as much deprived of mine as the poor negress in the slave market of New Orleans. And I dream sometimes even now of soft lips against my cheek, and little hands about my neck, which I never felt, which I shall never feel——Not even as a stranger shall I ever look again on——'

'The Czarovitch's son,' said d'Auban, with a strong rising in his heart. It was almost more than he could endure to hearken to this story in silence. He was more deeply moved than she could know. What it was a relief to her to tell, it was agony to him to hear. There are records of human iniquity and human suffering which fill the soul with a burning indignation, which wring it with an intolerable pity, which makes us bless God that we have never been tempted beyond what we could bear; that we have never been, like poor Charlotte Corday, for instance, maddened into one of those crimes which almost look like virtue.

D'Auban was thankful that day that the wide Atlantic rolled between him and the royal miscreant who had done such deeds of shame.

'A few more words, and then you will have heard all,' Madame de Moldau said, 'all that I can tell of the closing scene of that long agony of fear and suffering. I was continually warned of my danger: continually received messages to put me on my guard against eating certain food, or speaking alone to some particular person. The Czarovitch himself had often uttered dark threats, in which I clearly perceived the doom I had to expect at his hands. His hatred of me seemed to grow every day more intense. At last I discovered that a conspiracy against his father was on foot. Evidence of it fell in my hands. His mother, his sister, and his friends, as well as a large number of the Greek clergy, were engaged in it. I was thrown into strange perplexities. Whatever kindness I had received in Russia was from the Czar and his consort, and my soul revolted at the idea of being implicated in my husband's unnatural conduct.

' One day I took courage. We were alone together, which was not often the case. I told him of my suspicions, my more than suspicions of the plot he was engaged in. Oh! the look of his face at that moment! I dare not fix my thoughts on it. I remember every word he said, " that I had been his evil genius; that instead of marrying a woman he loved, he had been made to wed a pale spectre who had haunted him as the White Lady who foreshadows death in royal houses. That I hated his mother, and despised his church, but now the crisis was come. The day of doom at hand. The destinies of Russia were at stake. Swear," he said,

"Swear by God, that is, if indeed you believe there is a God—swear that you will be silent as the grave regarding the glorious delivery which is at hand. Do you value your life?" he said savagely, as I turned away from him without replying. "Do you value your life?" he repeated, his eyes glowing with an expression of mingled hatred and fear.

' "What has my life been that I should value it?" I cried, the strong sense of accumulated wrongs finding vent at last. "What has my life been but a living death since I set foot in this detested land, since I became the bride of a savage. Give me back my own country, give me back my youth——"

' " *Your* youth," he cried, " *your* country. Cursed be the day when you came from it, and stood between me and the true wife of my heart, and threw the cold shade of your sneers and your unbelief over the faith of holy Russia. But by that faith I swear you shall come this very day to my mother's cell and hear from her lips the duty of a wife." God forgive me! I was stung to the heart; I thought of what *that* woman had been, and of *my* patience and truth, and I murmured,

"Will *she* teach it me." My eyes doubtless spoke the sarcasm my lips dared not utter. He felled me to the ground. I remember the agony of the blow, I remember the look of his face, I remember my own wild cry, and then nothing more ; nothing for many nights and many days.

'When I recovered my senses I was, or fancied I was, alone. Lying on a small bed in a dark, low room, I saw nothing but stained whitewashed walls, and a small table on which were some bottles, and two or three common chairs. Gradually I called to mind, with that feeble groping sense of awakening memory, *who* I was, and then with a sort of bewildered astonishment wondered *where* I was. I had spent days of misery amidst splendour and discomfort, but so poor a chamber as this I had never even looked upon. With difficulty, and feeling faint and giddy, I raised my heavy head from the pillow, and saw M. de Sasse sitting near the stove warming his hands, and looking very ill. " M. de Sasse," I whispered. He started, and hurried to my side. " Where am I ? What has happened to me ? " '

' " You are *dead*," he emphatically whispered; " that is, everybody, and the monster who killed you, thinks you are dead." Who killed me? What monster? Ah! it all came back upon me, and I gave a fearful scream. " Hush, hush! for heaven's sake!" implored M. de Sasse. " Nobody must know you are alive."

' I pressed my hand on my forehead, for my thoughts were beginning again to wander. " Is there anybody near me but you ? " I said, faintly.

' " The Countess of Konigsmark will be here presently. She will tell you all that has happened. Try to sleep a little again." I closed my eyes, but I could not rest. " Is this the world to come? " I said. " It is like a horrid dream without a beginning or an end. It is very dark. Is it night or day? Is this life or death? " Then a nervous agitation seized me, I began to tremble and to weep. The poor old man bent over me imploring me to be silent. My sobs became loud and convulsive, and his face grew wild with apprehension. He laid a pillow on my face, and I cried out, " Will you, too, murder me?" I shall never forget his groan as he dashed the pillow to the ground, and tore his grey hair. Poor, faithful old man, it was the sight of his grief which quieted me. I gave him my hand and fell asleep, I believe. The next time I woke, the Countess de Konigsmark was kneeling by the bed-side; when I opened my eyes they met hers. I had known her from my earliest childhood. Her son, Comte Maurice de Saxe, had been my playfellow in former days. She was one of my few friends since my marriage. Whenever she came to the court of Russia, her society was a consolation to me. During those years of misery she was the only person to whom I opened my heart. What a relief it was to see her that day! I stretched out my arms, and she folded me to her breast.

' " I like this little dark room, now that you are here," I whispered. " I do not want to go away, if you will stay a little with me. And you, too," I added, turning to the old man, who was gazing wistfully at me from his seat near the stove. " Nobody cares for me in the whole world, but you two."

' " My darling princess," said the countess, " do you care to live ? "

' I started up in wild affright, a dreadful idea had passed through my mind. I was perhaps a prisoner condemned to death. " What have I done ? Am I to die ?" I cried, " Is the Czar dead ? "

' The tears fell fast from the countess's eyes. She shook her head; " No, but he is far away, my princess, and the wretch who all but killed you, and believes that he did so, would not have suffered you to live if he had known that you had escaped from the effects of his ferocity. I had the absolute certainty of this. His measures were taken, and I saw but one way of saving you. We sent him word that you were dead, and spread abroad the news of your decease. A mock funeral took place, and the court followed to the grave what they supposed to be your mortal remains."

' " It is very dreadful," I said, shuddering.

' " If it had not been for this stratagem your faithful servants could not have saved you. The Czarovitch has determined you shall die."

· "And he thinks that I am dead?" I asked, with a strange fluttering at my heart, such as I had never known before. "But when he hears that I am alive! Ah, I am afraid! I am horribly afraid! Hide me from him. Save me from him." I clung to the countess with a desperate terror.

'"We have concealed you," she said, "in this remote corner of the palace. M. de Sasse and two more of your attendants are alone in the secret."

'"I am still in the palace, then?"

'"Yes; but as soon as you have recovered a little strength you must fly from this country. We have all incurred a terrific responsibility who have been concerned in this transaction, for we have deceived not only the Czarovitch, but the Czar himself. The court, the nation, your own family, all Europe, have put on mourning for you. The funeral service has been performed over a figure which represented you, sweet princess; the bells have tolled in every church of the empire for the flower of Brunswick's line, for the murdered wife of the Czarovitch—for your supposed death is laid at his door."

' "I am dead, then," I exclaimed, looking straight at the countess with such a wild expression that she seemed terrified. "I am dead, then," I repeated again, sitting bolt upright in my bed, and feeling as if I was the ghost of my former self. "Am I to remain always here?" I asked, glancing with a shudder at the dismantled walls and narrow windows.

' "No," she softly answered. "Like a bird let loose, like a prisoner set free, you will fly away and be at rest." "Yes, yes," I cried, laying my head on her shoulder. "Rest— that is what I want." And my tears flowed without restraint.

' "Under a brighter sky," she continued, "amidst fairer scenes, you will await the time when a change of circumstances may open the way for your return."

' " Cannot I go to Vienna, to my sister, or to my own native Wolfenbuttel?"

' I immediately saw in the countess's face how much this question distressed her. "Princess," she said, "this is not possible. Not only the Czarovitch, but the Czar himself, believes you are no more. If you revealed your existence, you would expose to certain death those who, at the risk of their lives, saved yours. Besides, the Prince will never suffer you to live. His emissaries would compass your death wherever you went. I have evidence that you were taking poison in your food, and that it was only the antidotes I persuaded you to use which enabled you to struggle against its effects."

' "Then I have no hope left," I cried, " no possible refuge. It would have been better to let me die. Would that my husband's hand had dealt a heavier blow, and that the grave had really closed upon me!"

' "What! is there no charm in existence?" Madame de Konigsmark exclaimed. "Have you drained the cup of happiness during the twenty-three years you have lived? Cannot enjoyment be found in a life of retirement?"

' "Drained the cup of happiness!" I bitterly cried. "Why mock my despair? Have I known a single day of peace since I married the Czarovitch? Let me die of hunger, or call my husband's hirelings to despatch me at once, but do not drive me mad by talking to me of happiness.'

'I raved on for some time in this state, half conscious, half delirious, I believe, fearing to fix my thoughts on anything, and doubting whether those who had saved my life were my friends or my enemies. Madame de Konigsmark sat patiently by my side for hours together, watching, as I have since thought, every turn of my mind. She became more and more alarmed at the bold measures she had adopted, and seemed terrified lest I should refuse to disappear altogether from the world where I was known. Nothing could be more skilful or better planned than the way in which she brought me to the point. She did not say anything more on the subject that day, but on the following morning she induced me to rise from my bed, and led me to an open window looking on a garden at the back of the palace. The sudden burst of a Russian spring—the most beautiful though the most short-lived of seasons—was imparting a wonderful beauty and sweetness to the shrubs and flowers. The sky was of the softest blue, and a southern wind fanned my cheek, reminding me of my fatherland. It awoke the wish to live. I could not now bear the idea of dying, either by violence or by poison, the effects of which had already, in spite of antidotes, begun to tell upon my health. I felt incapable of forming plans, but to get away—to escape—became now my most intense desire. At nights I was afraid of assassins. Every sound—every step—made me tremble.

'A day or two later, Madame de Konigs-mark came to me in great alarm. One of the prince's favourites had been seen in the palace, conversing with the servants and making enquiries, which M. de Sasse had overheard. Rumours were afloat, she told me, that I had been killed by my husband, and my attendants, it was supposed, would undergo an examination.

' " Princess, you must go this very night," she said. " I will accompany you to the coast. M. de Sasse and one of your women will go with you to France. You can easily travel thence to America, where you will be perfectly safe from discovery. I have secured for you a sum of 50,000 roubles, which is by this time in Messrs. Frère's hands in Paris ; and all the jewels which are your own property you must take with you. M. de Sasse will pass for your father; ánd if Mademoiselle Rosenkrantz should decline to leave Europe, you can easily procure in France another attendant. There is not a moment to lose. Your own life, and the lives of all concerned, are at stake."

' The suddenness of the proposal took me by surprise. I seized her hands and cried : " I cannot forsake my son."

' " Alas ! " she answered, " have you enjoyed a parent's rights, or a parent's happiness ? Have you been suffered to be a mother to your child? He is safe in the Czar's keeping. He can protect him better than you could. Believe me, princess, if the Czarovitch discovers you are alive, I cannot answer for your life or for mine. Do you think I should urge you to forego your position if there were any other way of saving you ? "

' It was not difficult to persuade me ; I had not strength to resist. In the middle of the night we descended the narrow staircase, and found a carriage waiting for us. I moved like a person in a dream. Madame de Konigsmark was by my side. I do not remember having any distinct thoughts during that journey, or any feeling but that of a hunted animal pining to escape. When we came near to the coast, and I felt on my cheek the peculiar freshness of the sea air, it revived me a little; but when, by the light of the moon, I caught sight of the merchant vessel which I was to embark in, a sense of desolation came over me. My friend wept bitterly as she gave me a parting embrace. I did not shed a tear. It seemed as if everything within me was turned to stone. I sat down on my wretched cabin-bed; the anchor was raised and we began to move. For a long time I neither spoke nor stirred. The poor old man—once my servant, then my only protector—watched me all that day and the following night. I believe the first words I uttered were some that have often been on my lips since that time: " Free amongst the dead ! " '

' Free with the freedom of God's children ! ' d'Auban exclaimed. ' Oh, Princess ! what a miracle of mercy has your life been ! '

' I can see it now; but at the time all was darkness. From Hamburgh, where we landed,

we went to Paris, and soon afterwards to
Hâvre de Grace, where we embarked, as I
have told you before, in a vessel with eight
hundred German emigrants on board. I
was impatient to get away from France,
always fancying myself pursued by the
Prince's emissaries. Even at New Orleans
I was in constant fear of being recognised
and insisted on leaving it as soon as possible.
We only stayed till M. de Sasse could dispose
of my diamonds and had placed the money at
a banker's. Here I thought I should be out
of the reach of travellers. You can imagine
what I suffered the day those strangers
came. I could not resist the wish to hear
something about Russia and my poor little
son. Alexander Levacheff recognised me.
I saw him in private, and exacted from him
an oath of secrecy. And now I have only a
very few more words to say. Some persons
in our position, M. d'Auban, might feel when
about to part, "It would be better that they
had never met." But I can, and from the
depths of my heart I do say : "It has been
well for me that I have met you, known you,
trusted you——" '

She broke down, and could not finish the sentence.

He was going to answer, but she stopped him and said, with some excitement:

'But *you*—what good have I done you? I have saddened your life by the sight of my grief, long wounded you by my silence, and now I leave you. less able perhaps to bear your solitary existence than heretofore.'

He could scarcely speak. Men do not find words as easily as women, when they are deeply affected.

'It is true,' he said, in an almost inaudible voice. 'But, nevertheless, I am glad you came; I can say it with truth. Whatever I may have to suffer, I shall always thank God for having known you.'

'Well, it may be one day, on your death-bed, perhaps, a consolation for you to think that you have acted very justly and kindly towards one who, when she came in your way, was drifting like a rudderless bark on a dark sea. The Bible says, that man is blest who could have done evil and did not do it. I might well apply to you those other

words of Scripture : " Thou art that man."
May He who knows all reward you ! '

No other words passed between them.
He took her hand, silently kissed it, and
withdrew. The shades of evening had gradually fallen, and the moon was shining on
the long thick grass of the lawn. As he
looked upon the beautiful glade and the sil-
vered landscape, he thought of the night
when Thérèse had for the first time spoken
to him of the white man's daughter. As
long as he was listening to her he had hardly
realised what it would be to live and to
work on alone in that spot where for two
years she had been his constant companion
and the principal object of his life. Now it
seemed suddenly to come upon him. He
not only knew it must, but also felt it ought
to be. There was no prospect of escape
from this dreaded separation. It might take
place at any moment. Overpowered by his
grief, he sank on a bench in the garden, and
was only roused from his sad musings by
Simonette's voice.

'Monsieur d'Auban !' she said, in a loud
whisper.

'What do you want?' he exclaimed, starting to his feet.

'I have something to say to you. I want you to promise not to let my mistress' (it was the first time she had called her so) 'leave this place before I come back. And whilst I am away, please both of you not to grieve too much.'

'What—what are you talking about? What is it to me whether you go or stay?'

'Nothing, I know,' answered the girl, in a voice the pathos of which might have struck him had he been less absorbed by his own grief. 'But I am going away. Do not be harsh to me. Perhaps you may never see me again.'

'I do not know why you go. I cannot talk to you to-night. Leave me alone.'

'Will you not say a kind word to me?'

'For heaven's sake, go away!' cried d'Auban, scarcely able to command himself.

'Do not be cruel to me. I want all my strength for what I am about to do. I was within hearing just now, when madame was speaking to you. I heard what she said.'

'Good heavens! and do you dare to tell

me so?' exclaimed d'Auban, pale with anger. 'I have had patience with you long. I have shown great forbearance, but I shall not suffer you to remain here any longer as a spy on your mistress. She shall know of your base conduct.' He walked away, greatly agitated.

'Wait—wait!' cried Simonette, in a tone of anguish, and clasping her hands together. He did not turn back. She gazed after him for a moment. 'Not one look! not one word!' she murmured. 'Well, be it so. In the land of the hereafter there will be no scorn, no unkindness. Oh for strength of limb, and skill, and courage! Now for the spirit of my childhood—the fearless spirit and the brave heart! God and my good angel befriend me! The travellers to Canada cannot be here before the end of next month. My father says so.'

D'Auban passed a wretched night. He reproached himself bitterly for not having examined if it was indeed true that the French girl had overheard the Princess's story, and not taken measures to secure her secrecy. He felt his anger had made him

imprudent. He resolved to see her the very
first thing in the morning. But when, as
early as was possible, he went to St. Agathe,
Simonette was not to be found. Madame de
Moldau and the servants supposed she had
gone to the village. He went there at once,
but she had not been seen. He told Thérèse
she had spoken wildly the night before of
going away, and observed that she did not
seem surprised at her disappearance. Father
Maret, to whom he communicated all that
had passed the day before between him and
Madame de Moldau, and also during his brief
interview with Simonette, expressed his fears
that she had gone to New Orleans to de-
nounce her mistress as the possessor of stolen
jewels.

'She has often spoken to me of her scruples on that subject, and, not being able,' he
said, 'to reveal to her the explanation of the
mystery, she never seemed satisfied with my
advice to let the matter rest. If, however,
she did overhear the truth last night, it is
scarcely credible that she can have carried
out her intention. She may, however, have
heard the Princess speak of her flight from

Russia, and not the preceding facts—enough to confirm her suspicions, not enough to enlighten her. Would I had stopped and questioned her! The doubt is most harassing. But she cannot have started alone on a journey to New Orleans!'

'She is quite capable of doing so.'

'Would it be of any use to try and overtake her?'

'If even we knew for sure which way she has gone, we have no clue as to the road she has taken, whether by the river or through the thickets. The wild attempt may be fatal to her.'

'Full of risks, no doubt. But she is used to these wild journeys. I would give a great deal she had not gone, for more reasons than one.'

D'Auban's heart sank within him. Letters lately received from New Orleans mentioned that orders had been sent out by the French Government to make enquiries in the colony as to the sale of jewels supposed to belong to the Imperial family of Russia, and to arrest any persons supposed to be in possession of them. If suspicions previously existing were to be renewed by Simonette's depositions, the Princess might be placed in a most embarrassing position; it might lead to inextricable difficulties; and yet there was nothing to be done but to wait—the greatest of trials under such circumstances. Father Maret hoped the travellers to Canada would soon arrive. D'Auban was compelled to wish for it also. In the mean time he tried to reassure Madame de Moldau about Simonette's disappearance by stating she had hinted to him the day before that she had some such intention. Though with little hope of success, he despatched men in various directions, and one in a boat for some miles down the river, to search for her. At nightfall they returned, without having discovered the least clue to the road she had taken. The next day an Indian said that a canoe, belonging to her father, which was moored a few days before in a creek some leagues below the village of St. Francis, had disappeared, which seemed to confirm the supposition that she had gone to New Orleans. D'Auban suffered intensely, from a two-fold anxiety. He reproached himself for the harsh way in which he had spoken to

Simonette, and sometimes a terrrible fear shot across his mind. Was it possible that she had destroyed herself! He could not but call to mind the wildness of her look and manner. He knew how ungovernable were her feelings, and how she brooded on an unkind word from any one she loved. The blood ran coldly in his veins as he remembered in what imploring accents she had called on him to stop on the night he had left her in anger, and how she had said that the task she had to perform would require all her strength. Had she gone out into the dark night driven away by his unkindness, and rushed into eternity with a mortal sin on her soul—the child whom he had instructed and baptized, and who had loved him so much and been so patient with him, though with others so fiery! The bare surmise of such a possibility made him shudder, especially if at night he caught sight of something white floating on the river—a cluster of lotus flowers, or a branch of cherry blossoms, which at a distance looked like a woman's dress. But by far the most probable supposition was, that she had gone to de-nounce her mistress; and this caused him not only uneasiness as to the consequences, but the greatest pain in the thought that her affection for him had prompted this act, and that if he had had more patience and more indulgence it might have been prevented. Day after day went by and brought no tidings of the missing girl, nor of the expected travellers. Heavy rains set in, and even letters and newspapers did not reach St. Agathe and its neighbourhood. This forced inactivity was especially trying at a time when their minds were on the full stretch, and news —even bad news—would almost have seemed a relief. Since their last conversation there was much less freedom in the intercourse between d'Auban and Madame de Moldau. They were less at their ease with each other. Both were afraid of giving way to the pleasure of being together, and of saying what was passing in their minds. She was quite a prisoner in the pavillon. During those long weeks of incessant down-pouring rain, Simonette's absence obliged her to wait on herself, and she set herself with more resolution than heretofore to attend to household affairs, and to make herself independent of the services of others. She read a great deal, too, and almost exhausted d'Auban's small collection of books. He no longer spent the evenings at St. Agathe, but came there once a day to see if she had any commands. He did not venture, however, to absent himself for many hours together, for the fear never left him of Simonette's disclosures bringing about some untoward event. Week followed week, and nothing interrupted the dull, heavy monotony of the long days of rain, or brought with it any change to cheer the spirits of the dwellers in the wilderness.

END OF THE FIRST VOLUME.

LONDON
PRINTED BY SPOTTISWOODE AND CO.
NEW-STREET SQUARE.